Signs Point to Yes

SANDY HALL

Swoon Reads New York

A Swoon Reads Book
An imprint of Macmillan Publishers Limited

First published 2015 by Macmillan Children's Books
an imprint of Pan Macmillan
20 New Wharf Road, London N1 9RR
Associated companies throughout the world
www.panmacmillan.com

ISBN 978-1-4472-8671-4

1 3 5 7 9 8 6 4 2

A CIP catalogue record for this book is available from
the British Library.

Book design by Anna Booth
Printed and bound by CPI Group (UK) Ltd, Croydon CR0 4YY

For my niblings, from smallest to tallest,
Katie, Bri-Bri, Zak, and Billy

Chapter 1

JANE CONNELLY NEEDED A JOB, AND SHE NEEDED IT FAST.

Her mother was knocking on her bedroom door, calling through it, to tell her about the "great" unpaid internship she'd found for Jane at the university where she was an adjunct.

"It's in the American Studies department. They need some help with filing. You'd get fantastic experience, Janie," she said through Jane's locked door. "You'll need that for your college applications."

"I know, Mom," Jane lied. She *didn't* know. She wasn't sure she even wanted to go to college, and she had no clue what American Studies really entailed. It sounded awfully broad.

"What are you doing in there?"

"I'm changing my shirt," she said, holding a pillow up to her face so her voice would be muffled. That was how much she didn't want to have to face her mother at the moment.

"Well, come downstairs and talk to me when you're done changing," her mom said. Jane heard footsteps retreating down the hall and then coming back seconds later. "Are you going somewhere? Is that why you're changing?"

"No, Mom," she said. There was a good chance that the combined sighs of mother and daughter could be heard around the world.

Jane bolted over to her computer, needing to find something, anything, to do with her summer. Her two best friends were going to be counselors at band camp, the sleepaway kind. They were leaving the next day for their ten-week stint. But seeing as how Jane wasn't actually in the band, nor did she play an instrument, a job as a band camp counselor wouldn't work for her.

A quick Google search brought her to an online job board. She clicked fast and furious, hunting for any jobs that might suit her, scrolling through the ads as if her life depended on it.

As if being friendless for the summer wasn't bad enough, spending all of break at her mother's university sounded like the opposite of anything she was interested in. It sounded soul sucking and mind numbing. So maybe, in a way, her life *did* depend on it.

★ Telemarketer: part time, unlimited earning potential
★ DO YOU LOVE DOGS?! Min. wage but get to play with puppies!
★ Knives, Knives, Knives: excellent commission

- ★ **CASH FOR BILLS!**
- ★ **Sperm donors needed**

Each one was worse than the last.

Her parents would kill her if she got involved in a pyramid scheme; she knew that for a fact. Her older sister, Margo, had gotten involved in one a few years ago. She was trying to sell beach condos. In their beach-adjacent community. The worst part was that her parents never seemed to get mad at Margo for the pyramid scheme. They claimed the humiliation of losing her money was punishment enough. Jane disagreed, but no one ever asked her.

"Margo skipped a grade. Margo passed all the AP tests with the highest marks. Margo got a full-time internship at Princeton University this summer, and she doesn't even go there. Margo's going to be the first person on Uranus," Jane muttered under her breath. In a moment of desperation, she clicked on the link for *Child Care*. It was a last-ditch option, but that was where she was; that was what her life had come to.

Jane scanned the listings, knowing that she needed to avoid any and all situations that involved babies. Babies were terrifying, with their soft spots and their wobbly necks. Way too much responsibility for a girl like Jane.

- ★ **Mother's helper needed for newborn triplets.**
- ★ **Child care in our home.**
- ★ **Do you love babies?**

★ Babysitter needed.

She clicked on the last one because it was located in her town.

She skimmed it once and then slowed down to scan it more closely on the second read-through.

Four days a week, 9 to 5 . . .

Eek. Nine a.m. was not her best time of day. But it was in town, so she wouldn't have to get up too early to make it there on time.

As long as it was within walking distance.

Jane's parents had given her a hand-me-down car for her seventeenth birthday, but of course Margo was using it to drive to Princeton every day. Margo's internship was far more important than Jane's technical ownership of the vehicle. Maybe if Margo had actually made some money in that pyramid scheme, she would have money to buy her own car.

What made the situation even more frustrating was that Jane could never even complain about it. Her parents would point out that Jane wasn't paying for the car herself, and therefore it was still theirs. But if Jane mentioned something along the lines of the fact that Margo had her own car in high school that she didn't have to share with anyone, she would be met with stony-faced silence. To Jane, it was the principle of the thing. It was a double standard.

She sighed and went back to reading the ad.

Three girls—a set of five-year-old twins and a seven-year-old . . .

Sounded exhausting but also doable.

Fifteen dollars an hour . . .

It might not be the easiest job on earth, but that was decent money. Even Jane's allergic-to-math brain told her it was close to five hundred dollars a week. Five hundred dollars a week was always better than zero dollars a week. And she wouldn't have to spend extra time with her mother.

There was no name with the advertisement, so Jane composed the e-mail "To whom it may concern." She stated her name, phone number, and babysitting experience—which was limited to watching her cousins during family events, but she could probably get her aunt to fudge their relationship if she needed references.

She held her breath, crossed her fingers, rubbed her lucky rabbit's foot, and hit Send.

Jane checked the clock and knew she needed to talk to her mother. If she didn't go downstairs to talk to her mother, then she definitely needed to study for her finals. Her last two finals were the next day, and Jane needed to show her teachers the old razzle-dazzle if she wanted a grade higher than C in either of those classes.

She weighed her options, then decided on a third: none of the above.

Instead, she went back to reading the *Doctor Who/Little Women* fan fiction she'd started the previous evening.

The blossoming love between the Eleventh Doctor and Jo March was some of the most fascinating reading she'd ever done. Particularly because she could never deal with Jo marrying the German guy. How could she do that with Laurie right next door?

Jane was about to get to the *good stuff* when her cell phone rang. She considered ignoring it in favor of the good stuff, but it was an unknown number and her curiosity was piqued.

"Hello?"

"Jane!" an unfamiliar voice said in a very familiar way.

"Hi?"

"It's Connie Garcia-Buchanan." Once she heard the name, Jane realized that she should have immediately recognized the voice, with its slight Spanish accent and permanent smile.

"Hello," she said, still confused that Connie was calling on Jane's cell phone. "Do you want to talk to my mom?"

"No, sweetheart! I got your message about the babysitting job. I was very surprised to hear from you, but so happy."

"Oh," Jane said, still not quite catching on.

"The girls just adore you, and I think you would be great with them this summer."

"Oh! Oh my God," Jane said, slapping her forehead in shock. "I didn't realize. I just thought . . . Well, I didn't think. I didn't put it together. It's an anonymous ad. . . ." She stumbled and stammered, trying to grasp what was happening.

"I understand. I thought for sure you had put it together, what with the girls and their ages. And the job being here in town."

Jane laughed because she was uncomfortable, and that was what she did when she was uncomfortable. She also felt incredibly stupid. But that wasn't new for her.

"It would be nice to have someone so close by," Connie continued while Jane sat on her bed and chewed her nails down to the quick.

"Yes, that makes sense," she said.

"I'm getting my master's degree in social work—I don't know if your mom mentioned that to you. I decided to take three classes this summer, trying to get ahead of the game. Two of them are offered online, but I didn't realize what a beast it would be trying to entertain the girls while I did homework and studied for exams. Not fun."

"Not fun," Jane said, slightly dazed.

"When are you done with finals?"

"Tomorrow," Jane said. She tried to keep a smile in her voice even as the reality of the situation sank in.

"Can you come over around four o'clock? For an interview?"

"Um, yes. I guess so." Jane tried to ignore the thought gnawing at the edge of her brain.

"Good. I promised the girls they could help choose their babysitter. So while I don't feel like I need to interview you, they're still going to want to."

Connie laughed, so Jane did, too, but it sounded like "ha ha ha" rather than actual laughter sounds a normal person would make. She loved Connie and the three little girls. She even thought Connie's husband, Buck, wasn't too bad a guy.

"And I would only need you until the beginning of August. Classes end after that, so you would still have a few weeks off before school starts."

"That would be great," Jane said. She tried not to think about the real problem. But the more she tried not to think about it, the less she could ignore it.

"I'm so happy you're one of the applicants. The other ones were a little less than desirable. A few were downright creepy."

"I guess you never can tell who might crop up from an online ad."

"That's for sure," Connie said. "Well, this is great. So great. Thank you so much for applying, even if you didn't know it was me you were applying to."

"You're welcome."

"I'll see you tomorrow at four, then."

"See you then."

"Excellent. Say hi to your parents for me."

"I will."

Connie paused before saying good-bye.

"And, Jane, I know you and Teo don't talk much anymore, but this will be so good for the girls. Don't let anything from the past stop you from making choices in the present."

There was a solid chance that Jane died of embarrassment right there on the phone. What were the odds that she accidentally, anonymously applied to babysit for Teo Garcia's younger half sisters?

Margo would know the odds, the little voice in the back of her brain said. She told it to shut up, but it never did.

When Jane regained her composure and came back from the dead, she said, "Thanks, Connie. I'll keep that in mind."

"Bye, Jane."

"Bye." Jane tapped the End button on her phone and flung herself back onto her bed, rolling around, trying to figure out what she had gotten herself into.

Connie had it wrong, though. Teo wasn't the problem. Teo was a nice guy, if not slightly boring. The problem was his constant shadow and Jane's eternal foe, Ravi Singh.

What Jane could never understand was why a guy like Teo Garcia had a best friend like Ravi Singh.

Only one thing would be able to soothe her at the moment. She picked up her trusty Magic 8 Ball and considered what question to ask.

"Is it a bad idea to take this babysitting job?" Jane asked the Magic 8.

Cannot predict now.

Definitely not the answer she was looking for.

Chapter 2

Someone tapped on Teo's bedroom door so lightly that he barely even heard it. This usually signaled that his sisters were playing in the hallway. They had all sorts of games that Teo didn't know the rules for and they wouldn't explain to him.

A light tap on the door was always supposed to be met with him throwing the door open and yelling "boo" or growling or doing something to make them giggle.

Today he pulled the door open and yelled, "Gotcha."

Unfortunately, he found his stepfather, Buck, on the other side.

"Sorry," Teo said, straightening up. "I thought you were going to be Keegan."

"Oh, got it. Sure. Keegan's always up to something."

Teo nodded.

Buck nodded.

They stood there for a moment.

"Um, so did you need something?" Teo asked.

"Oh. Yeah. I was wondering. Well, your mother and I were wondering, if you wouldn't mind, maybe."

Teo bit his lip and fought the urge to close the door in Buck's face. He wouldn't go so far as to say that he didn't like Buck, because most of the time they got along okay. Things would be easier with Buck if he would just say things to Teo rather than beating around the bush so much.

"Is this about the lawn?" Teo asked.

"Yes," Buck said, visibly relaxing.

"Mom already talked to me. I'll mow it. She said I could do it this weekend after I was done with school." Teo gestured toward his bed, where all his AP chemistry notes were laid out. "My last final is tomorrow."

Buck looked into his room and let out a low whistle.

"Gotcha," he said. "Well, that's a good boy, then."

Buck patted him awkwardly on the back, but he didn't move to walk away.

Teo smiled, tight-lipped, and closed the door, just to have Buck tap on it again.

"I, uh, wanted you to know that I appreciate all your hard work, and I'll give you twenty bucks for a good job."

Teo paused. He was saving every last dime he could so he wouldn't have to live with his mom and Buck again after graduating from high school. But sometimes money from

Buck felt tainted or as if he was bribing Teo. Still, money was money.

"Thanks, Buck," Teo said.

"You're welcome." He continued to stand in the doorway.

"I'm going to shut the door now, okay?"

"Oh, yeah, good luck with studying," Buck said, and then he finally, *finally*, walked away and Teo could get back to the solitude of his room.

Life would actually be easier if Buck lived up to some kind of evil-stepfather stereotype instead of being this squirming, wishy-washy people pleaser.

When Teo was younger, he thought Buck's issues were because Teo was Puerto Rican and Buck was white. But as the years passed, it became obvious to Teo that it had more to do with their age difference.

Buck was uncomfortable having a stepson only fifteen years younger than he was, and it wasn't Teo's job to make him feel okay about it. So now there were these big, gaping silences and a deep crevasse of awkwardness between them. The older Teo got, the weirder things were.

He shot his friend Ravi a whiny text about Buck, but Ravi didn't answer immediately, so Teo was going to have to find some other way to amuse himself. He stared at the notebooks on his bed and sighed. He had too much work to do for Buck to distract him this way.

Teo really had only one choice. In order to restore balance in his life, he did a quick Google search for *Jose Rodriguez*.

It was his favorite fantasy, meeting his father and his father's family. Anytime things got weird with Buck, Teo would start his search all over again. He had never met Jose, but that didn't keep his imagination from running wild.

The problem was, Teo didn't know much about his father besides his name and that he was Puerto Rican. Teo tried searching a couple of different combinations of his parents' names together and got tons of hits because their names were common, but nothing useful or concrete. He wasn't sure what he would do if he ever found his father. Mostly Teo wanted to know where his father was. Knowing that he was out there somewhere would be enough.

The doorbell rang downstairs, and Teo heard the murmur of voices filtering up through the air-conditioning vents. *This must be another one of the potential babysitters*, Teo thought. There had been a whole train of them in and out of the house all week.

He listened for a few more minutes to the muffled voices coming up from the living room. The more his sisters giggled, the more curious he became.

He checked his phone again—still nothing. Where the hell was Ravi? He almost always answered his texts within minutes.

Carefully, Teo cleared his search history and x-ed out the tabs. His nightmares often featured a scene where Keegan asked something along the lines of *Who is Jose Rodriguez?* during dinner. *Teo was looking for him on the Internet*, she would continue.

Then his mom, Buck, and all three sisters would stare at Teo until their eyes popped out onto the dinner table and rolled around. Nightmare Teo could speak only Spanish, and not even Nightmare Mom understood him. Not being understood was a theme in a lot of his recent nightmares.

Checking his phone one last time, Teo tiptoed out of his bedroom and sat at the top of the stairs to eavesdrop as his sisters interviewed the Potential Babysitter with a constant barrage of inane questions.

"Do you like brownies?" Piper asked.

"What kind of brownies?" Rory asked before the Potential Babysitter could even reply.

"Will you make brownies with us?" Keegan asked.

Their rapid-fire dessert questioning didn't surprise Teo. They were passionate about baked goods.

"We could make brownies," the Potential Babysitter said.

"Yay!" all three girls cheered.

"See?" Rory said. "I told you she'd be nice."

"So what will you let us do?" Keegan asked.

Teo knew that question was like the kiss of death. As the oldest of the three girls, Keegan tended to be the ringleader. She was the kind of kid who, if you turned your back to her long enough, would rally the rest of the kids and start a mutiny. He knew this for a fact, as she had already done it once when she was in kindergarten and twice in first grade. Teo's mom spent a lot of time in parent-teacher conferences about Keegan.

Teo checked his phone again.

"What do you mean?" the Potential Babysitter asked.

"Like, can we go to the pool, and the sprayground, and mini golfing?" Keegan clarified.

"I guess?" the Potential Babysitter answered.

"The mini golf at the boardwalk?" Piper asked. "Not the dumb one on the highway."

"Yeah, that one's for babies," Rory added.

Teo had no idea how they came up with those kinds of rules, but they were forever evolving. Last time he checked, they loved the mini golf course on the highway because it was fairy-tale-themed.

"We'll have to ask your mom about that," the Potential Babysitter said. Teo knew his mom would like that the girl was deferring to her in these matters.

All three girls started talking at once. This would be a make-or-break moment for this poor girl.

"Mom never lets us go to the boardwalk."

"Maybe you could tell her to take us."

"Or maybe Teo could take us."

Teo slid down a few steps and peeked through the slats of the handrail. He couldn't see the face of the girl they were interviewing, but he really wanted to interject that he would *not* be taking anyone to the boardwalk.

"I want to play the crane machine."

"I want to play Skee-Ball."

"I want to mini golf."

"I want to go on the log flume!"

The storm of wants and requests kept raging. Teo felt legitimately sorry for the Potential Babysitter at this point. He was surprised that his mother hadn't stepped in to help. She must have wanted to see how the older girl would handle all three kids when they got whipped into a simultaneous frenzy.

"Do you guys like Slip 'N Slides?" the Potential Babysitter asked over the din.

The three girls all grew quiet. "What's that?" Rory asked.

"It's kind of like a log flume for your body." Teo thought that was an excellent description of a Slip 'N Slide.

"Really?" Keegan asked.

Teo leaned over again to watch the proceedings.

The Potential Babysitter nodded.

"Do you have one of those?" Piper asked.

"Yup. In my garage."

"What else?"

"Um. Well. Okay." She rubbed her palms on her shorts. "We could set up the sprinkler and one of those little wading pools and make a fountain. We could turn the lawn sprinklers on, and it would be like having our very own sprayground."

Teo smiled. He used to do stuff like that all the time at the Connellys'.

And that was when he realized his sisters were interviewing Jane Connelly. The girls were all going wild about the setup that Jane had described, and Teo tried to back up the stairs, instead knocking his elbow hard and hissing in pain.

"Teo?" Keegan asked, walking over to the steps.

"Crap," he said under his breath.

He played it cool and walked down the stairs the rest of the way like a normal person.

"Hey, guys," he said. He turned to Jane and nodded at her casually.

"Hey," Jane said.

"You remember Jane, right, honey?" his mom asked. She was sitting at the dining room table, observing the interview.

He opened his mouth to say something snarky like *How could I forget Jane?* Then he thought better of it. Instead, he shot his mom a look as he passed that he hoped she would interpret as *You could have warned me.*

Thankfully, his phone vibrated at that moment. Finally. Wait until Ravi heard what was going on.

Ravi

> Eh, don't worry about Buck.

> You should invite me over for dinner.

"Um, gotta take this," he said to the room at large, not focusing on anyone, as he wandered into the kitchen and leaned against the counter.

He tapped out a message to Ravi, telling him to come over for dinner, and continued to listen to his sisters interview Jane. He felt trapped and regretted that he hadn't stayed in his room.

The girls peppered her with questions.

"We can go to the library and on picnics. We can take walks and ride bikes," Jane said.

The thing about Jane Connelly wasn't so much that Teo didn't like her. He was neutral about her. She was always nice enough to him. He had spent a lot of time with her while his mom was taking night-school classes.

But Ravi hated her. He claimed she was his archnemesis. Teo didn't see it, but he also wasn't interested in fighting with his best friend about a girl who didn't really matter.

It would suck to have Jane around all the time. Ravi would be so pissed off. He practically lived at Teo's house in the summer because his parents refused to put on the air-conditioning unless it was over a hundred degrees outside, and Ravi couldn't handle that.

Maybe Teo's mom wouldn't hire Jane. There was still hope.

But hope died moments later when he heard his mom offer the job to Jane, who accepted it on the spot.

Of course.

Teo took a deep breath, preparing to tell Ravi the news. His fight-or-flight response kicked in, which was really more like an all-flight, all-the-time response. Conflict was not his forte. He would rather go back to studying chemistry than tell Ravi this news. Maybe they would never be at his house at the same time, and Ravi would never have to know the truth.

But the thought of Ravi coming upon Jane in the kitchen one morning after a sleepover, and the yelling that would ensue, was enough to force Teo to suck it up and tell him.

> Jane Connelly is going to babysit my sisters this summer.

Ravi's answer was immediate.

Ravi

> THAT IS THE WORST NEWS I HAVE EVER HEARD. I AM GOING TO HAVE TO HAVE A LONG TALK WITH CONNIE ABOUT THIS DECISION. HOW COULD YOU LET THIS HAPPEN?

> You know how my family is. There was no way I was going to be asked my opinion.

> BUT SERIOUSLY. JANE CONNELLY OF ALL PEOPLE!?

> You need to chill out with the caps lock.

The next five words came in separate texts.

Ravi

> I

> WILL

NOT

CHILL

OUT!

Teo let out a long breath. This wasn't going to end well.

Chapter 3

MARGO HAD ONE THOUGHT ON HER MIND ALL DAY, ALL WEEK, even all month if she was being honest with herself. There was one thing that was keeping her up at night, making her feel guilty, and taking up a lot of brainpower. She kept telling herself that ripping off the Band-Aid would feel so much better than dealing with the pit in her stomach and her clammy palms every time she thought of this one particular thing: finally coming out to her parents.

They were nice people. They wouldn't disown her for being bisexual. At least that was what she told herself over and over again on her way home from work every day.

She thought about different ways to come out. Maybe write them a heartfelt note or perhaps hire a skywriter.

She grinned, thinking about that one as some butthead

nearly sideswiped her car. Jane wouldn't be pleased if Margo hurt her precious 1998 Buick LeSabre. It seemed like every driver on the road was out to get her, always honking at her and giving her the finger. Like she was *trying* to get into a car accident.

Margo was happy every day she made it home alive, and today was no different. She pulled up in front of the house and sighed with relief.

As she walked through the front door, she accidentally let it slam behind her, alerting the lady of the manor to her presence.

"Margo, is that you?" her mom called from the kitchen.

"No, Mom. It's a burglar."

"A burglar wouldn't call me Mom."

"I know, Mom. It's a joke."

"Oh," her mom said, sticking her head around the corner. "Dinner will be ready in fifteen minutes. Let your sister know. I don't want her to be shocked when she's forced to come downstairs for dinner."

Margo would have laughed, but she felt for Janie. Sometimes it seemed as if her mom and her sister couldn't agree on anything, not even something as simple as dinnertime.

Margo trudged up the stairs and dropped her stuff off in her bedroom before peeking through the slight opening of Jane's bedroom door.

"Hey," Margo said, opening the door a little further.

"Hello," Jane said, her voice dull.

"Mom wanted you to know that dinner will be ready soon."

"Cool."

Margo glanced around the room. "Why do you have a poster of a blue phone booth?"

"It's not a phone booth. It's a police box," Jane said.

"What's up?" Margo asked, leaning on Jane's desk. There was an odd feeling in the room. Jane was curled up on her bed, staring into the corner of her room.

"It's kind of a long story," Jane muttered.

"We have at least a few minutes before Mom forces us to eat dinner."

Jane smiled at that. Their mother loved staying on schedule.

"She's going to kill me," Jane finally said.

"I'm probably going to need further information to decide whether you're exaggerating."

"Mom got me an unpaid internship at the university, and I went out and got myself a babysitting job instead."

Margo *tsk*ed. "Yeah, Mom's gonna be pissed."

"Thanks for your support," Jane said, flipping over facedown on her bed.

Margo took a seat on the bed and patted her sister's back awkwardly. "You know what I mean."

"I do."

"So why'd you do it?"

Jane rolled over and sat up. "Probably because the idea of driving to and from work with Mom every day basically sounded like hell."

Margo nodded. "She really does like to get on your butt about things."

"Can't you ever say 'ass'?"

"She really does like to get on your *ass*," Margo repeated.

"Thank you. It sounds better that way. Like you're actually on my side."

"I am on your side."

Jane frowned. "I don't think anyone is really on my side."

"So where's the job?" Margo asked, rather than arguing with Jane's statement. She knew it would only end with Jane going off on a tangent about how the rest of the family were geniuses and Jane was a poor little imbecile. She'd heard it all before.

Jane shook her head. "That's kind of the worst part. At the Buchanans'."

"Shouldn't that be good news?"

"I don't know. When I asked the Magic 8 about it, it seemed hesitant."

"How can the Magic 8 seem hesitant?"

Jane handed the toy over to Margo. "It kept telling me to ask again later."

Margo closed her eyes and held the ball, concentrating on the question or else she knew Jane wouldn't accept the ball's answer. "Will Mom flip out on Jane?"

Margo looked at the answer and read it out loud. "'*Ask again later.*'"

"Maybe it's broken," Jane said.

Their mother called them for dinner then, interrupting Margo's answer.

"What were you two doing upstairs?" their mom asked when they came into the kitchen to fill their plates.

"Girl talk," Margo said with a grin toward Jane as they took a seat at the table.

"Where's Dad?" Jane asked.

"In the basement. He's worse than you two." She stood up from the table and called through the basement door for her husband to come eat before the pork got cold.

Once everyone was seated, Jane took a deep breath. "I got a job," she said.

"Yes, Jane," her mom said. "At the university."

"Um, no, a different one. Connie—you know Connie around the corner—needed a babysitter for the girls this summer. She's taking a ton of classes and, well, I got the job. I'd really like to help Connie out."

"That's nice of you," her dad said, smiling genuinely, obviously oblivious to his wife's unhappy glare.

"I got Jane an internship at the university this summer, Steven. It's going to look great on her college applications."

"The pay is really good," Jane continued. "I don't have much savings, and the job Mom found is unpaid."

"You know, Linda, maybe Jane finding a job on her own is a good thing," he said pointedly.

"Maybe she needs to be more concerned about her future and less concerned about making money," her mother said.

"Or maybe she needs to do what she enjoys." Her father's eyebrows went into his hairline—that was how hard he was trying to make this point.

Jane sank back into her chair, looking relieved. Her mother leveled her gaze at her.

"Do you really want this? It's going to be hard, much harder than filing. Being a babysitter isn't as easy as it looks. Especially for kids as energetic as those Buchanan girls."

Jane sat up straight. "I want to. I swear. I went over there yesterday, and they interviewed me. It seemed like a lot of fun."

"Fun?"

"Yes, fun. Even if it is hard work, it seemed like it could also be a lot of fun. And the girls seemed so excited."

"All right."

"All right, I can do it?"

"Yes," her mom said. "It's good that Connie will have some reliable help this summer. From what she tells me, Teo is in a funk. Being rude and always out with that boy."

"What boy?"

"That Ravi. The one who used to always tease you so much in middle school."

"Thanks for the reminder, Mom."

"Maybe he liked you," her dad said.

Before Margo had a chance to tear into him about how sexist and awful it was that boys could tease girls under the auspices of "liking them," her father stood and started clearing the table, and her mother followed. Margo's rant would have to wait for another day. Along with any chance for her to come out.

Even if her parents had stayed at the table, there was no way she could have come out to them after that display. It would have been foolish to even try to talk to them when they both had Jane on the brain.

Or at least that was what Margo told herself so she would stop feeling like such a coward.

She would come out when the time was right, on her own terms.

"I need to get back downstairs," their dad said. "I'm working on a huge submarine model, and I'm at the trickiest part."

Margo rolled her eyes but helped with clearing the table.

Only Jane sat there through the cleanup, looking stunned.

Margo took the seat across from her once everything had been put away and the dishwasher was humming.

"It sucks that Mom acted like that," Margo said when their mother had slipped out the back door to take the trash to the garbage cans.

"Thanks," Jane said. "But it actually went way better than I'd expected. She didn't even mention me quitting. I thought for sure that would be her fix for everything."

"What would you have done?"

Jane looked thoughtful. "I would have really pushed the whole 'helping a neighbor' angle. She would have eaten that up. I think luck was on my side, though, since mom had talked to Connie recently."

"True," Margo said.

"I wonder what's up with Teo. I thought he was always some kind of perfect son."

"Yeah, perfect Teo, always doing what his mom needs him to do, never complaining."

"He practically ruined our childhoods by being so perfect. And now he's off with Ravi Singh, making trouble every night."

"Wait, has Teo really gone all bad-boy?" Margo asked.

"No. I don't think so, at least. It's probably more along the lines of Mom totally misconstruing something Connie said and turning the fact that he's not home much or whatever into a much bigger deal than it is."

Margo squinted. "Yeah, I just really can't imagine what kind of trouble those two would even get into."

"I bet they mug old ladies."

"And knock over mailboxes with baseball bats."

"Take candy from babies," Jane said.

"Hot-wire cars," Margo added.

"Drink wine coolers and stay out past ten."

"Yeah, they're totally badass."

Jane pumped her fist in the air. "Yes! I love it when you curse."

Margo giggled at her sister's enthusiasm for swearing.

Margo almost told Jane her secret right there in the dining room. It had been a long time since she'd felt this close to her sister. Sometime in her teens Margo had lost touch with Jane, and then when she left for college, she never seemed to have the time. But maybe this summer would be a good chance for them to become friends again.

It couldn't hurt to have one.

Unfortunately, their mother came back in from the yard, and their dad starting yelling from the basement, and the moment was lost. But Margo promised herself that she would find another one and not let it pass her by.

Chapter 4

ON HER FIRST DAY OF WORK, JANE SLIPPED OUT THE FRONT
door with a yelled good-bye toward the back of the house.

"But what about breakfast?" her mom called from the kitchen.

"I'm not hungry." Jane slammed the door good and hard to
punctuate that sentence.

She ate a granola bar that she found at the bottom of her
backpack and washed it down with water from the bathroom
sink. It might not be the most balanced breakfast, but it got
her out of the house nice and fast.

She marched down the street and around the corner, proud
that she was actually going to be twenty minutes early. If only
school were this close to her house, she might be early for that
sometimes, too.

Connie had told Jane to let herself in the back door when she arrived, because it was sometimes hard to hear the doorbell from inside the house, and Connie wanted Jane to get comfortable streaming in and out anyway. Connie had had a key made for her and everything.

So Jane let herself in through the back door and was met by a shirtless Teo in the kitchen.

If she were a different kind of girl, she would have let out a wolf whistle.

For the record, she'd seen him without his shirt plenty of times in the past. He was the kind of guy who would mow the lawn without a shirt on or would whip it off while playing soccer with his friends. He was a lifeguard, for God's sake, Jane told herself. She'd seen his naked torso on numerous occasions.

But somehow, while he was sleep-mussed and standing in his own kitchen wearing only a pair of basketball shorts, it was a completely different story.

She tried to calculate the last time she'd seen him without his shirt on and realized it was probably last summer. Jane would guess he'd done a lot of abs work during those long winter months, because she could basically count his six-pack.

"You're early!" Teo said, putting down his glass of orange juice and covering himself with a paper towel.

Jane turned away to hide her laughter and the blush that was traveling up her entire body, only to walk directly into a kitchen chair.

"Sorry," Jane squeaked, apologizing to Teo and the chair she knocked over.

"No, it's cool. Just a little surprising," Teo said, looking at the paper towel as though he wasn't entirely sure how it had gotten in his hand. He put it down, then went into the laundry room and grabbed a sleeveless T-shirt, pulling it over his head as he reemerged.

"Thanks. I obviously can't handle the sight of boy nipples," Jane said, blushing even more deeply and slapping her hand over her mouth. *I shouldn't even be allowed to speak*, she thought.

Teo's eyes went wide, and he blushed as deeply as Jane had.

She squeezed her eyes closed and balled her hands into fists.

"What are you doing?"

She carefully opened one eye so she wouldn't totally lose her concentration. "I'm trying to sink through the kitchen floor."

"Oh, yeah, sure."

"Any advice?"

"I've never actually sunk through a floor before," Teo said, but now he was smiling, and Jane could at least relax a little.

Jane cleared her throat. "So, um . . ."

"Teo," an annoyingly familiar voice said from the basement stairs, "I thought you were bringing down Pop-Tarts."

Jane thanked all the gods she could think of that someone was about to rescue her from this embarrassing moment.

Unfortunately, that someone was none other than Ravi Singh.

He took one look at Jane, and then, making a production of ignoring her, he turned to Teo. "What's for breakfast?"

"Good morning to you, too, Ravi," Jane said.

"Oh, Jane, how lovely to see you," Ravi said with the kind of fake grin usually reserved for creepy clowns in horror movies.

Teo just stood there with his mouth open. He had backed himself into the doorway. Jane figured he wanted to be able to beat a hasty retreat if she and Ravi went nuclear on each other.

"You want a Pop-Tart?" Ravi asked Teo, holding the box he had found in the pantry and offering one to him but not to Jane.

Truth be told, Jane did want a Pop-Tart, but she certainly wasn't going to ask Ravi for one as if she were some kind of peasant asking for a boon.

"I need to get out of here," Ravi told the room. "I have SAT prep this morning. I need to get my score up if I'm serious about applying to anywhere Ivy League."

Jane rolled her eyes and tried not to regurgitate her granola bar.

"How did *you* do on the SATs?" Ravi pointedly asked Jane, stuffing half a Pop-Tart into his mouth.

Lucky for Jane, he wasn't the first person she'd had to dodge on this matter. "I did perfectly fine for where I want to go."

"And where do you want to go?" Ravi asked, gesturing with the other half of his Pop-Tart. "I think you'd be good with one of those HVAC repair programs, or maybe a gas station attendant."

"Gee, I don't know, *Mom*. Maybe wherever you aren't?"

Teo snorted and Jane looked over at him, shocked. Ravi usually tossed insults at Jane, and Jane took them while Teo stood idly by, ignoring their back-and-forth.

As Jane was about to go on, feeling bolstered by Teo's seeming appreciation of her level of wit, all three of his sisters came spilling into the kitchen.

"Jane, Jane, Jane!" they all said at the same, each of them trying to tell her something different.

Buck walked in then, too, and patted Teo on the back.

"You're looking good this morning," Buck said to Teo, squeezing his biceps on one arm. "Did you start using heavier weights, like I suggested?"

Jane would have died on the spot, but Teo seemed to take his stepfather's words in stride, even if he curled in on himself a bit, crossing his arms and stepping away from Buck.

Jane would have liked to stay and listen to the rest of the exchange because, damn, she should be getting exercise tips from Teo, and maybe Buck, too, if he was the genius behind Teo's new body. Unfortunately, the girls were all desperate to take her to the basement and show her various toys.

"Mom said we had to wait for the boys to wake up," Keegan explained, taking Jane's hand and walking down the carpeted stairs. "We wanted to wake them up, but she wouldn't let us."

The large basement had two separate areas, one with a TV and a sectional couch, where the floor was piled high with blankets and pillows from the sleepover. Beyond that, an area in the back was sectioned off with shelving that held all the girls' toys, including a kitchen set that Jane would have gone wild for as a kid.

The girls got deep into playing almost immediately, and Jane joined in. She tried to focus their play on the kitchen area, because, really, it was beautiful, but they seemed to want to play a game that, from what Jane could gather, was essentially My Little Pony DMV. There was a pony behind a couple of blocks in a pile, and the other ponies would step up and ask questions about insurance coverage.

They didn't even really want Jane to play, because every time she picked up one of the figures, they would tell her that now Applejack (or whoever) had to go to the end of the line because Jane had made her lose her spot.

Connie came down to say good-bye to the girls.

She tsked at the mess that the boys had left in the basement and told Jane not to clean it up for them. "They're big boys. They can handle it."

It hadn't even crossed Jane's mind to clean it up.

Connie asked Jane to come back upstairs so they could go through the regular schedule.

Today would be easy because the girls only had swim class at eleven. "I tried to keep it light to start with so you could get used to the routine and get to know the girls a little bit better," Connie said.

"Thanks," Jane said, trying to peek around to see if muscle-man Teo was still lurking.

"Do you feel okay about driving the minivan?"

"Yes."

"And make sure the girls are all strapped into their seats before you drive. Sometimes they like to pretend they buckled themselves in, and then they climb into the front

♥ *35* ♥

seat and scare the bejesus out of me."

"That sounds terrifying."

Connie nodded and smiled. "If you need anything, text or e-mail me. Even when I'm in class, I can usually get back to people that way. But the girls are really self-sufficient. Try to be at least within earshot of them, but you don't need to be on top of them all the time."

Jane nodded. She could handle that.

"Feel free to bring along a book or a magazine or summer homework or anything," Connie said. "I know you're giving up a lot of time to be here, so I don't want you to feel like you have to watch them every second."

Jane smiled because that was very good news. She had totally planned to watch them every second.

"And if you're hungry, take whatever you want from the fridge or the cabinets. Let me know if there's anything you like that we don't have. Especially lunch-wise, since you'll need to feed yourself and the girls every day."

Connie must have caught Jane's scared look. "It doesn't have to be anything elaborate. Sandwiches, fruit. Rory doesn't eat bread. She's not allergic or anything—she just doesn't eat it—so I make her cheese roll-ups or crackers with peanut butter."

Connie finished packing her bag and let out a deep sigh. "All right. I'll see you around five!" she said.

Jane went back down to the basement and kept an eye on the time, but it seemed to be moving in the wrong direction when the girls decided they wanted to play hide-and-seek. They would hide and Jane would have to find them. And according to the girls, all games of hide-and-seek had to be started from the living room.

Jane threw open the basement door at the top of the stairs and felt it crash into someone.

"Ah!" Teo's voice came from behind the door.

The girls slipped around Jane and out of the basement while Teo stood there rubbing his exposed toes in his flip-flops.

"I'm so sorry!" Jane said. "I thought you'd already left for work."

"It's cool. It's not a big deal. I didn't need those particular toes," he said. "Crap, I never cleaned up the basement, did I?"

Jane shook her head, and Teo glanced at the time on his phone.

"It's cool," Jane said. "I'll clean it up. It's the least I can do, since I just hobbled you. The girls will help. Right, girls?"

They looked blankly at Jane.

"Don't you want to help Teo out?" she asked them.

They looked at her, and then at Teo, and then at one another before they started dancing around and yelling, "Yes! We love to help!"

"Yeah, we'll take care of it for you. After we play hide-and-seek."

Teo grinned and squeezed her shoulder. "Good luck with hide-and-seek, and I totally owe you one. Thanks."

Jane smiled as she stood in the living room with her eyes closed and counted to fifty, as the girls had instructed her. If Teo was going to be a nice guy this summer, it would definitely help balance out the pain of Ravi.

When Jane got to fifty, she yelled, "Ready or not, here I come!"

Checking upstairs first seemed like a good idea, since she hadn't heard the door to the basement open.

Buck had done a lot of work on the house over the years, putting on an addition and reconfiguring the layout. It was like a completely different home. Jane was met with a long hallway of closed doors when she got upstairs, and she tried to listen for giggles, but there was complete, eerie silence.

Maybe the girls hadn't gone upstairs; maybe they went outside to hide, even though Jane had told them outside was off-limits. Or maybe they had left completely and were on their way to Acapulco, for all Jane knew.

She tried to imagine breaking the news to Connie and Buck that somehow she had lost all three children while playing hide-and-seek on her first day. After the court trial, there would be a made-for-TV movie about the girls: *Hide-and-Seek Gone Horribly Wrong: The Story of the Buchanan Sisters.*

After prowling the hallway, listening for any sound of the girls behind the closed doors, she decided she needed to be more systematic in her approach. She would open each door and check under the beds and in the closets. After that she would check the basement.

The first door she opened was obviously the twins' room. Two beds to check under and just a tiny closet. Next was Connie and Buck's room. She scanned it fast because it felt totally wrong to be in there. Unfortunately, they had a rather large walk-in closet that required extra effort.

After that there was the bathroom, where she looked behind the shower curtain and then in the linen closet. Unless the girls had climbed onto a shelf and perfectly replaced all the folded towels and sheets in front of them, she could definitely cross off the linen closet with one quick look.

The next room was Teo's. She really didn't want to be in Teo's room, but she had to check for the girls, because now she was getting a little nervous.

She bumped her hip on his computer desk, and the screen came alive. She didn't mean to look at the search bar, but her eye was drawn to it.

How to find your biological father, it said.

Jane gasped and put her hand over her mouth. This was not information that she should be privy to. Immediately she x-ed out the window, and a second one was open behind it. *Consuela Garcia and Jose Rodriguez*, the search said in that window. She closed that one, too, and backed out of the room, shutting the door and fleeing back downstairs, trying not to think about what she'd just seen.

The girls were all sitting at the kitchen table, eating grapes.

"You didn't come find us," Keegan said.

"I was looking for you everywhere upstairs," Jane explained, taking a grape for herself and sitting across from the girls.

"We were in the basement."

"I thought for sure you would have hidden under a bed or in a closet."

Rory looked terrified. "That's where the monsters live."

Jane laughed. "Good to know," she said. "How did you get downstairs without the door making any noise as you opened and closed it?"

"You have to do it really slow," Keegan said.

"Also good to know," Jane said as she focused on the kids, determined to forget that she had ever been in Teo's room.

Chapter 5

BARELY TEN MINUTES INTO HIS SHIFT, TEO HAD A SINKING feeling in his gut like he forgot to turn off the stove. But it was worse than potentially setting the house on fire, because he was pretty sure that what he'd forgotten to do was clear his search history. He paced around the pool, trying to remember exactly how the morning had played out.

He'd been so humiliated by Buck's mention of his workout regime that the second Ravi left for SAT prep, Teo ran upstairs to his room to do more dad searching, this time starting with something broader. Obviously, other people had searched for their biological fathers, and maybe Teo was trying too hard to reinvent the wheel.

It wasn't long before he'd looked at the clock and found that he was going to be late for work if he didn't get his crap together.

He'd left as quickly as humanly possible, and he really couldn't remember if he'd closed out his search or not.

He was so desperate for his mom or the girls not to see it that he almost considered calling Jane and asking her to close up the tabs for him. But then Jane would ask questions—questions Teo didn't want to answer. He was starting to sweat just thinking about it. He ran a hand through his hair and tried to rationalize the situation.

No one really went in his room all day. It could happen, though. But his computer would probably go to sleep after a while, and unless someone purposely woke it up, he would be fine. He didn't think Keegan really had it in her to be that nosy, and the twins couldn't read that well yet.

The good news was that Jane and his sisters would arrive at the pool in mere minutes for swim class. Surely he would know right off the bat whether Jane had found out his secret. Or, worse, whether Keegan had fulfilled his nightmarish prophecy of reading his search results. Wouldn't he?

When Jane came through the pool gate, she waved at him and didn't seem particularly fussed, or like she had learned his secret that morning. At least he hadn't been looking at porn, he told himself. But he found little comfort in that thought.

The pit in his stomach grew.

Teo watched Jane walk over to the covered seating after having made sure the girls joined the right groups. Rory was still in a state of distress because she was in a lower group than Piper and Keegan were, but she needed to learn that swimming wasn't something to fool around with.

Jane sat down next to a girl Teo knew from school but wasn't really friends with. *Claudia Lee, that's her name*, he thought. Teo tried to read Jane's lips as she was talking to Claudia. Not that he expected her to gossip with Claudia Lee about his personal dad-searching business, even if she *had* snooped on his computer, but still, he didn't really know Jane all that well.

He couldn't figure out how Jane knew Claudia. Jane ran in a crowd of dorky, less smart girls. She was like a band geek who wasn't in the band. Unless maybe she *was* in the band. Teo honestly wasn't sure. He couldn't even remember the last time he had talked to Jane at school, or even really noticed her there. Maybe when they'd ended up sitting next to each other at the drunk-driving assembly the year before.

He really didn't want Ravi's crazy anti-Jane propaganda to get to him. While he and Ravi were playing video games last night, Ravi wouldn't shut up about how terrible Jane was.

"I swear to God, she is the stupidest girl I've ever met," Ravi had said out of nowhere.

"Who now?" Teo had asked, mostly to annoy Ravi. He'd known exactly who Ravi had been talking about, but he sort of got tired of listening to the same old, same old from him. Sometimes he liked to mix it up and ask all the wrong questions.

"Jane Connelly. She's dumb."

"How do you figure?" Teo asked.

"'Uh, really, Ravi,'" Ravi said in a voice that Teo assumed was supposed to be Jane's. "'I don't get it. How do the ducks know where to cross?'"

"She never asked that."

"Sure she did."

"It was probably meant to be a joke, but you have no sense of humor whatsoever."

"I swear she asked it in driver's ed last year."

"So is this really how we're celebrating the end of school?" Teo asked. "Sitting in my basement, bitching about Jane Connelly?"

They had changed subjects after that, thank God, because Teo couldn't handle much more of Ravi's Jane-bashing.

The thing was, there wasn't anything wrong with Jane. And he actually had a newfound respect for her after this morning. Not only had she totally ignored how ridiculously embarrassing Buck was, but she'd also offered to clean up the mess in the basement. In his book, that made her a decent person.

Maybe he should just talk to Jane, see if she acted like she knew his secret.

The problem was that Claudia Lee was a friend of this other girl Megan. Teo had gone out with her a few times last year. They were in a lot of the same classes and were both on the forensics team. She was on the girls' soccer team and he was on the boys'. It made sense for them to go out. But things had fizzled between them, and Megan had been bitter, and now having to approach Claudia could definitely be awkward. He got enough of that at home these days.

But unless he wanted to spend the rest of the day panicking, he didn't have much choice.

"Hey," he said, approaching Jane and Claudia when swim class was over.

"Hey," Jane said, squinting up at him.

"Yo," Claudia said.

"How are you guys?" Teo asked, looking at each of them in turn.

"Peachy," Claudia said.

"Good. Nothing has really changed in my life in the past couple of hours," Jane said.

Teo looked at her intently in an attempt to decipher if she seemed sort of shifty or like she was trying to hide something.

"I was telling Jane that my dad and stepmother are basically blackmailing me to bring Dinah and Job to swim class all summer."

"Oh yeah?" Teo asked, half listening, half examining Jane's body language.

"Yeah, I want to go to this superexpensive art school in Chicago, so they said that if I could save them money by being Dinah and Job's nanny this summer, they would put all that toward school."

"Sounds like a good deal," Teo said. At this point, Jane was staring back at him with a confused expression. She couldn't know. But what if she knew? The little voice in the back of Teo's head wouldn't let it go.

Claudia was barely containing her laughter. "You guys should just kiss already."

"Um," he said, looking from Claudia to Jane. "What?"

"What? Oh my God," Jane said, covering her face.

Teo's eyes went wide. "Us?" he asked.

"Yeah, you've been staring at each other this whole time."

"Uh, no." Teo backed away a step.

"Uh, *yes*," Claudia said.

Jane stared at the pavement, and Teo felt terrible.

"Hey, Jane," Teo said, hoping to break the tension. She looked up at him through her eyelashes. "Any chance you know how to sink through concrete?"

She started laughing.

Just then the girls came skipping over with several of their friends, including a little girl who Teo realized was probably Claudia's stepsister.

"Look at what Dinah made!" Keegan said, showing Jane and Teo a folded-up piece of paper.

"Claudia taught me," Dinah said proudly.

"Oh, that's a cootie catcher," Jane said.

"Yes! A cootie catcher," Rory said. "It catches all the cooties and locks 'em up and throws away the key."

Jane nodded seriously at this description. "It's for telling fortunes," she explained.

"Yeah, it's the funnest. We like telling fortunes," Piper said.

"You know," Teo interjected, leaning into the little crowd, "Jane used to be awesome at this stuff. She was really into Magic

8 Balls and tarot cards. And she used to make the best cootie catchers."

Jane blushed a little, Teo thought, but it could have been the sun getting to her.

"Really?" Keegan asked. "Can you make one for each of us?"

"Of course," Jane said.

"Jane knows all sorts of stuff like that. About superstitions and cool myths."

"I do?" Jane asked.

"Yeah, you were always telling me to hold my breath when we drove past graveyards and not to step on any cracks in the sidewalk."

"Really? I don't remember."

Teo shrugged. "You made an impression. I have never opened an umbrella in the house, nor will I ever."

Jane laughed again.

Piper pulled on the hem of Teo's shirt, so he knelt down to talk to her.

"How do you know Jane?" she asked.

"When we were kids, her mom used to babysit me sometimes while our mom went to work."

"Really?"

"Yup."

"You were friends?"

"Sure," Teo said.

"Are you still friends?" Keegan asked. She had a talent for making things awkward, much like her father.

"Um, yes," Teo said, smiling over at Jane, hoping she would play along. In kid world, their passing acquaintance would probably be called friendship, even if they never talked to each other, spent zero time together, and mostly avoided each other at school. Although Teo knew that it was partially his fault for always being around Ravi.

"Of course," Jane said.

"Do you ever have playdates?" Piper asked.

Claudia snorted. Teo had kind of forgotten she was still sitting there.

"Not anymore," Jane said. "Moms don't really set up playdates for kids in high school."

Piper nodded seriously.

Claudia and her stepsiblings left a minute later, and Jane started getting the girls ready to go home.

"Hey," Teo said, putting his hand on Jane's arm. "I wanted to thank you again for offering to clean up the basement for me. That was cool of you."

"Yeah, no problem. We haven't done it yet, because we needed to get ready for swim class. But I figure I'll trick the girls into doing most of it by telling them it's a race."

"You have quite the devious mind, Jane Connelly."

"I'll take that as a compliment."

After work, Teo was happy to find that the basement was in perfect shape. Not only that, but he had been wrong: He *had* closed out his tabs from earlier that morning. He hadn't wiped his history, but at least the dad search hadn't been sitting there for the whole world to see.

It was also nice to know he had an ally in Jane. Now he just had to try to get Ravi to stop antagonizing her, and they'd be in pretty good shape.

Chapter 6

ON JANE'S SECOND DAY OF BABYSITTING, SHE MADE THE girls a huge pile of cootie catchers. They spent most of the morning before swim class making up creative fortunes to write inside them.

" 'Your babies will look like puppies,' " Keegan said.

"That's not very nice," Jane said. "You don't want babies to look like dogs."

"But puppies are cute!"

"They are," Jane said. "But I think we can do better."

" 'You will get a puppy'?" Rory said.

"I like that one," Jane said, writing it down.

Jane worked on creating a long list of ideas because the girls wanted to make unique cootie catchers for each of their friends and Teo.

"What should we put in Teo's?" Jane asked.

"'You will marry Jane so she can be our sister,'" Piper said.

"Wow, thanks, guys. But I don't want Teo—"

"Teo is going to marry his girlfriend, Megan," Rory said.

"Teo has a girlfriend?" Jane asked.

"Not anymore," Keegan said. "He told Mom they broke up a long time ago."

Jane wasn't sure what "a long time ago" was in kid time, but it got her thinking: She never heard much about Teo and girls. Not that they were exactly in the same social circle, though.

They were the same level of dork at their school, just at opposite ends of the spectrum. Jane was band dork adjacent, and Teo was a kind of smart, sort of athletic dork. In fact, if he didn't hang out with Ravi, who was mostly just too smart for his own good and had a tendency to turn people off, Teo might even have been popular. He was cute and on the soccer team. Jane had to wonder if he actually chose his dork status.

When she and the girls got home from swim class, Jane was not thrilled to find Ravi on the back deck, reading a book and acting like he owned the place.

"Jane," he said, not even trying to hide his air of disdain while Teo wasn't around.

She rolled her eyes and corralled the girls into the house—except for Piper, who decided to sit on the deck and give Ravi the third degree. Jane listened through the screen door.

"What are you reading?"

"*The Jungle.*"

"Why?"

"For school."

"What's it about? Tarzan?"

"If only," Ravi said.

Jane found it kind of fitting that Ravi got along better with a five-year-old than he did with most of his peers. Except for Teo. He obviously really liked Teo.

"Time for lunch," she said to Piper through the screen door. Piper scampered inside, and Jane stepped out onto the deck, shielding her eyes from the sun.

"Teo won't be home from work until four o'clock," she told Ravi.

"Like I don't know my best friend's work schedule," Ravi said, shaking his head. And then a devilish expression flitted across his face. "Any chance you want to bring me a drink? Maybe make me some lunch, along with the girls?"

Jane shook her head slowly, staring at Ravi to drive the point home.

"I'll take that as a no."

Jane raised an eyebrow and then turned to go back in the house.

"So that's definitely a no, then. Maybe I'll just order a pizza."

Jane gritted her teeth but said nothing. She had a headache just thinking about Ravi hanging around the house for the rest of the afternoon. Or, even worse, the rest of the summer.

As Jane set out the girls' sandwiches, Keegan said, "We

should invite Ravi in for lunch."

"Ravi is fine."

After checking and rechecking the schedule, Jane saw that the girls had no activities for the rest of the afternoon, so she was going to have to come up with something for them to do while also resolutely ignoring Ravi. She'd rather not hang around the house and have Ravi insult her all day.

"What do you guys want to do after lunch?" Jane asked, hoping beyond hope that they would have a good idea.

"Can we play with sidewalk chalk in the driveway?" Piper asked.

"Of course," Jane said, relieved that it wasn't a backyard activity.

"Awesome. Ravi is the best at drawing with sidewalk chalk," Rory said.

"Did I hear my name?" Ravi asked, sticking his head through the door and smirking at Jane.

"You wanna play sidewalk chalk with us?" Keegan asked.

"You know it," he said, walking into the kitchen and surveying the table. "Now, who wants to be a good sharer and let me have a piece of their sandwich?"

Each girl gave him half her lunch. Jane felt sick to her stomach as they marched out the front door to play.

"Do you really need to be here?" he muttered as the girls dumped their bin of chalk onto the driveway.

"I'm sorry. Where would I go?"

"Inside? Somewhere else? Home?"

"This is my job. You do realize that, right?" Jane asked, crossing her arms.

"Maybe it should be *my* job."

Jane rolled her eyes.

"I mean, if you're doing it, obviously anyone could do it. A trained monkey could probably do it," Ravi said.

"Look, we don't have to be friends, and we don't have to talk—"

"You're the one who started talking to me."

Jane narrowed her eyes. Obviously, Ravi had started this conversation, but if he was too delusional to remember something he'd done a minute ago, that wasn't her fault.

"Come on, Ravi," Keegan said, handing him a piece of chalk.

He set to work making the girls the most epic hopscotch court. Jane would have been impressed if anyone else on earth had made it. It was huge. He was making little doodles and drawings in the boxes. The girls loved every second of it.

Jane decided to go in the house and grab the notebook she used to plot fan fiction. She might as well make use of the time.

It was on her way back out of the house that Jane heard a cry and ran toward the driveway.

Rory was sitting on the ground holding her knee, and Ravi, rather than doing anything useful, was raking his hands through his hair and spinning around in circles.

"Hey, Rory," Jane said calmly, kneeling down next to her. She gave Ravi a dirty look. "Hey, hey, what happened?"

"I fell down." She sniffled.

"She tripped over her hopscotch rock," Keegan said.

"Can I see?"

Rory showed Jane her knee. It was scraped, but not too badly.

"Why didn't you tell me you went in the house?" Ravi asked.

"I was inside for literally two and a half seconds."

"Literally, Jane? Literally? No human moves that fast."

"Why didn't you try to check her knee?"

"'Cause blood skeeves me out," Ravi said.

Jane didn't have time for Ravi's phobias.

She picked up Rory and took her into the house, followed by the other two girls and, unfortunately, Ravi. He lurked while Jane cleaned Rory's cuts. Rory calmed down once Jane put a Band-Aid on her knee and kissed it "all better." Rory's sisters let her pick out a movie, and then they all climbed onto the couch together to cuddle.

Ravi stood in the doorway of the bathroom while Jane washed her hands. He still looked awfully pale.

"You okay?" Jane asked. "Not that I care. But I would rather not clean up your puke."

Ravi opened his mouth and Jane braced for the worst. "You're really good at that."

"At what?"

"At taking care of them."

"It is my job," Jane said pointedly.

Ravi started slow clapping. "I pay you the first compliment of your entire life, and you don't even thank me. Stay classy, Jane."

He turned on his heel and went out to the back deck.

All Jane wanted was to curl up on the couch with the girls, but she needed to deal with Ravi, no matter how unappealing that sounded. It was time she stood up for herself.

"If you're going to be hanging out here all freaking day, you could at least try to be helpful with the kids," Jane said as she walked out the back door.

He lifted his chin defiantly. "Aren't they your responsibility?"

"Yes."

"You gonna share your money with me if I help out?"

Jane sighed. "You know that's not what I mean. Like the very, very least you could have done was kneel down and make sure Rory was okay. You don't like blood—that's fine. Talk to her. Calm her down. You don't have to do anything with the blood. They obviously like you. I get that you can't stand me, but couldn't you at least be nice to them?"

The confrontation was making Jane shake. She'd been watching the girls for only two days, and she already loved them and wanted the best for them. Ravi acting like a complete useless jackass when one of them fell really pissed her off.

"Dude, chill out," he said.

"I'm perfectly chill, thank you," Jane said. Ravi's response was a really good example of why she hated confrontation. The way the other person could so quickly take the upper hand, no matter how righteous you felt about the situation, made her so angry. "I don't really understand why you're here when Teo isn't. It's weird."

"Because my parents don't put on our air-conditioning—"

Jane cut him off. "You're sitting outside, dumb ass. You could sit outside at your own house."

"Are you telling me to leave?"

Jane crossed her arms and took a deep breath. "Yes. Please."

"Hell, no. This isn't your house."

"But it is 'my responsibility,'" Jane said, making air quotes.

"I'm not gonna leave unless one of the people who actually lives here tells me to."

"Oh, we'll just see about that!" Jane said.

Jane went back inside and closed the kitchen door, locking it behind her. She could barely contain her rage. What had been minor shaky hands a few seconds ago now felt like full-blown spasms. She opened and closed her fists and tried to calm herself.

The last time Jane remembered having had the nerve to confront anyone quite like that was . . .

Never.

She'd never done anything like that before. She was like a mama bear protecting her cubs. She finally understood all those stories about mothers who were able to lift cars to save their kids. She cared about Rory, Piper, and Keegan so much she was willing to stand up to Ravi for them.

She didn't actually have any effect on Ravi, but that was a mere detail in the scheme of things. For once she had said what she was thinking.

By the time Teo got home an hour later, Jane had worked herself into a fit of worry and anger. Ravi had left once he realized that Jane had locked all the doors. But she knew that now she was headed toward a confrontation with Teo. She really didn't think she could handle two confrontations in one day.

The girls were watching *The Lion King* for the billionth time while Jane paced in the kitchen, wringing her hands and waiting for Teo to come in.

What if Connie heard about all this and thought Jane was acting like a big baby? Ravi was Teo's friend; he was allowed in the house if he wanted to be there.

Teo came in the back door.

"Hey," he said, smiling.

"Hi. I'm sorry."

"For?"

"For what happened with Ravi today."

"I don't know what you're talking about."

"I'm sure he's left a boatload of messages about it for you."

Teo fished his cell phone from the bottom of his bag and checked his texts.

"Oh. Wow." He scrolled and scrolled and scrolled. Teo's face was shocked, but his voice was still kind. "He is *not* happy with you."

"I'm really sorry. I didn't mean to start a fight. You know how he is with me," Jane said.

Teo looked at her, his face soft, almost sympathetic. "Yeah, I know."

"He was here for so long and I ran inside for a second and

Rory fell," Jane said.

"Is Rory okay?" Teo asked, looking concerned.

"Yeah, she's fine, but Ravi was such an ass about it." Jane paused and bit her lip. "I'm sorry, I'll stop calling your best friend names."

"No, please, feel free. He called you a whole slew of different things in these text messages."

Jane's heart dropped. "I don't think that makes me feel any better."

"Oh!" Teo exclaimed. "Yeah. That wasn't very nice of me. But I meant, don't feel bad. And don't apologize again. I don't really know what he was doing here. If my mom had been home, he wouldn't have been hanging around the house."

Jane nodded. "I'll be cooler from now on. I promise."

Teo tapped out a message and hit Send. "You shouldn't have to be. Here, look."

Jane leaned over to read the text Teo had sent Ravi.

Teo

> Dude, just stay home when I'm not here, then.
> And leave Jane alone. She's doing her job.

Jane bit her lip to keep her smile from getting too wide. "I don't even know what to say."

"No big deal."

"No way, it's a huge deal. Thank you so much." She felt lighter, like all her worries were dissolving.

"You're welcome. I should have said something to him a hundred years ago."

"What do you think he's going to say back?"

Teo's phone buzzed. "'Stop being such a fart nugget and take my side,'" Teo read.

"Wow, a fart nugget. That's. Wow. Inventive." Jane giggled. "I really don't want to start trouble between you guys."

"Nah, I can take it. And Ravi can, too. He's blind to the idea that not everyone appreciates his charms."

Jane sighed. "I know he doesn't appreciate my charms—hence, I avoid him."

"I think he wants to piss you off."

"Why, though? Why put out so much energy on someone he obviously can't stand?"

"Search me," Teo said with a shrug.

"What did you write back?"

"I'm not a fart nugget, he needs to stop coming over while you're here, blah blah blah."

"Any response?"

They waited for the phone to buzz again, and when it did, Teo was fast to check it.

"'Stop being an asshole. Why are you defending Jane?'" Teo read. And then he typed his message back, saying it out loud as he typed. "'You're the asshole. I'm defending Jane because she's doing a good job and I don't want my mom to fire her for killing you.'"

"Really, Teo. Thank you so much. I never could have done that."

"You hold your own with him."

"I do? I always feel like I'm just falling into his expectations for me."

"Nah, you do a good job."

"Thanks. But I really don't think he would have listened to me."

"No worries, Jane. I got your back."

Jane hesitated, unsure how to respond to that, unsure of how to show her gratitude for what Teo had done for her. She settled on patting his hand, which was weird and made her feel like her grandmother, but it was the only thing she could think to do.

"You have no idea how much that means to me," Jane said after a few seconds. She pulled and folded her hands on the tabletop, hating that she felt like crying. "And for what it's worth, I have your back, too, if you ever need me."

"For what it's worth, I really appreciate that," Teo said, his smile reaching his eyes this time.

They made eye contact for a second too long before they both looked away, blushing and making up excuses to leave the kitchen that very second.

Chapter 7

THIS FIRST THING THAT POPPED INTO **J**ANE'S MIND WHEN SHE woke up was Teo. She hadn't been able to stop thinking about him all weekend, so it was no wonder that he was waiting at the edge of her mind on Monday morning.

With all the time he spent with Ravi, it was apparent that Teo idolized his friend. Jane would have never guessed that he would ever tell Ravi off on her behalf. It made her feel like she could deal with all of this. And like she had made a new friend.

As kids, Teo and Jane had spent a lot of time together simply because their moms were friends. Jane never considered that they might actually be compatible people. Even if it was just friendship compatibility. It wasn't like Jane had too many friends. She was doing okay, but she could always use more.

Maybe Teo could, too.

The whole time she got dressed and ate breakfast, Jane was distracted, thinking about Teo standing up for her. She barely even heard her mom's words of caution about the stormy weather they'd be having all day.

At the last second her mom thrust an umbrella into her hands, thankfully. Otherwise Jane would have had to run, unprotected, to the Buchanans' in a downpour.

"Guess there won't be any swim class today," Jane muttered as she picked her way through puddles and around the corner. She went over the schedule in her mind, thinking of what kind of moods the girls might be in that morning. Buck was away on business, so that might throw them off a little, but at least they had story time at the library to look forward to that afternoon. Jane could divert their attention until then.

She ran around to the back of the house, not wanting to drag mud through the living room. And even though she knew it was ridiculous, there was no way she would bring an open umbrella into the house, so she stood under the awning to close the umbrella and lean it against the deck railing before slipping through the back door.

Teo was in the kitchen making breakfast for all three girls.

"Hi," Jane said, surprised but not unpleasantly so. She rubbed her arms to warm them. It was the kind of weird summer morning when she could have used a sweatshirt.

"Morning," Teo said.

"What's up?" Jane asked.

"My mom's alarm didn't go off, so no one woke up until my boss called to tell me that the pool would be closed for the morning."

"Am I late?"

"Nah. It was one of those things where she was so frazzled she ended up being ready to go early, so she asked me to watch the girls for a few minutes until you got here. She was worried about traffic."

"Ah, okay," Jane said. "Um, thanks for helping out. She could have called me to come over early. I feel bad if you have stuff to do." She took the empty seat next to Teo and leaned her elbows on the table.

"No, I'm cool."

"How about you guys?" she said to Keegan, Rory, and Piper. "You're awfully quiet this morning."

"They're not fully awake until they've had their Frosted Flakes," Teo said to Jane in a stage whisper, bumping his shoulder against hers.

Thunder rolled across the sky, and lightning crackled through the kitchen window. All five of them stared out the window. Every hair on Jane's body stood on end. She could barely stop herself from running around the house, turning off all the electronics and unplugging anything that could possibly be unplugged.

"You don't like storms, right?" Teo asked, as if reading Jane's mind.

Jane made a face. "I kind of hate them."

"We'll protect you," Keegan said, getting out of her chair and coming over to pat Jane's hand. Piper and Rory also stood up and hugged Jane from either side.

"You guys aren't scared?" Jane asked, trying not to outwardly quiver with each rumble of thunder.

"Daddy said that the lightning is outside and can't get us inside."

Jane didn't tell them what a complete lie that was. She assumed Buck wasn't trying to teach them proper lightning safety precautions and was probably just trying to calm their worries, but still. No wonder they weren't freaked out. They had been lied to. Because what the lightning really wanted to do was fry their brains and burn their house down.

Jane looked over at Teo, who rolled his eyes.

"I miss Daddy," Piper said.

Rory stopped hugging Jane and went over to hug her twin. "He'll be back soon, Pipe."

"I don't want to break up this lovefest, but are you guys done eating?" Teo asked.

"Yes," Keegan said.

"Lovefest," Piper said, giggling, already cheered up from missing Buck.

"I think you all need to sit back down and take the same number of bites as your age," Teo said.

The girls listened obediently and took the required number of bites before leaving the table.

The storm had passed for the time being, so Jane figured she should probably do her job and actually interact with the children in her care. "What are you guys going to do this morning?" Jane asked.

"Play in the basement!" Piper said, throwing her fist in the air.

"All right. I'll be down after I help Teo clean up."

Keegan, Piper, and Rory marched downstairs, and Jane turned to Teo.

"I'm really impressed with the bites thing. I'll have to remember that one."

"Don't be too impressed," he said. "My mom does it with them. I have very little authority where they're concerned."

"I wanted to thank you again for what happened with Ravi the other day. That was, like, the nicest thing anyone has ever done for me." Jane winced. She hadn't meant for that to come out quite so pathetically.

"It's cool. He's kind of pissed at me." Teo wasn't looking at Jane, instead studying the insides of the cereal bowls that he was rinsing out before putting them in the dishwasher.

"I'm sorry," Jane said.

"I'm not very good at, like, well, fighting with people."

"Ha. Yeah. I was kind of thinking the same thing."

Teo looked at her questioningly.

"About me. I'm the worst at that stuff. My palms get all sweaty, and I never say what I want to say."

Teo smiled. "Yes! I'm so freaking bad at confrontation. I feel like a wimp. I never walk away feeling satisfied."

"Well, if you can't feel satisfied for yourself, feel satisfied on my behalf."

Teo leaned his hip against the counter and turned to look at Jane. "For the record, I hold about as much authority over Ravi as I do over my sisters. He could still come back."

Jane shook her head. "Why, though? It's so weird."

"I don't know. Maybe he doesn't get enough attention at home."

Loud screams that Jane and Teo could no longer ignore were coming from the basement.

"I'm terrified that they're going to want to bake brownies this morning. They were so passionate about it when I was being interviewed that I didn't want to tell them I don't actually bake. Ever."

Teo scratched his ear and smiled. "Quite the conundrum."

"It is. How am I going to entertain them all morning?" Jane asked as Teo followed her down the steps. "Not to mention that if another storm comes through, I might actually become paralyzed with fear."

"What do you normally do in the morning?"

"Usually swimming tires them out until lunchtime, and then my job is basically to make sure they don't fall asleep standing up."

They walked into the main area of the basement and saw that the girls had made a mess. An unbelievable mess, considering they'd been down there for only about five minutes.

"All right," Teo said. "We need to come up with some way to focus their energy. I have an idea, but it will require you to keep them down here for another half hour."

"I think I can handle it," Jane said. "I hope I can handle it."

Teo patted her shoulder and ran up the stairs two at time. Jane turned to the girls, trying to ignore how warm her shoulder felt from Teo's simple, and completely friendly, touch.

"Teo is making a surprise for you upstairs," Jane said.

"Is it brownies?"

"No," Jane said. "But you have to help me clean up down here before we're allowed to go upstairs."

The girls turned into whirling dervishes, picking things up and putting them back into their proper places. In no time the basement had returned to its organized state and Teo was coming down the basement stairs.

"You guys ready for some fun?" he asked.

"Yes!" all three girls yelled, jumping up and down.

"Then come upstairs so I can present you with the Brand-New, Beautiful Buchanan Mini Golf Course!"

The girls galloped up the stairs and into the kitchen, where Teo had laid out the first hole. He handed each of them a small plastic golf club and a Ping-Pong ball.

The course was laid out through the entire house: up the steps from the kitchen, all through the second floor, and then down the steps into the living room. Teo had used all sorts of household items, and the girls went bananas for it. They were off and playing before Jane could even blink.

"This is incredible, Teo," Jane said. "I have no idea how I'm going to make this up to you. You keep doing these awesome things."

He shrugged. "It seemed like something they would be into."

"It's brilliant."

Thunder rumbled closer again and Jane flinched. The girls didn't even seem to notice this time.

"You would have come up with something on your own."

Before Jane could respond, lightning flashed close to the house.

"I think the only game I could have come up with this morning was 'stay under your bed to hide from the storm.' And that wouldn't have been fun for anyone."

Teo smiled and squeezed her arm again. "Then it's a very good thing that I was here."

The girls were still giggling and trying to get their Ping-Pong balls up the steps.

"That's gonna be a really tough hole," Jane noted, trying to distract herself from the storm.

"I'll let them walk the balls up the stairs once they get tired of it. I needed to make sure there were enough challenges to keep them busy."

Jane looked over at him and felt a funny little swoop in her stomach. Teo was trying to stick his hands into pockets that he didn't have. She grinned when he noticed her watching his awkwardness.

"Oops," he said, shrugging it off and blushing.

They followed the girls along the course, and by the time they finished, the sun had come out. Teo's boss called from the pool, and he had to go in to help open up.

"At least it'll be a shorter day than usual," he said, smiling.

"I like how cheerful you are." It was a compliment Jane might have felt embarrassed to give someone else, but something about Teo made her want to acknowledge everything she liked about him.

"Thanks," he said, blushing and shrugging again. It was like he couldn't stop shrugging around Jane.

"I should make the girls some lunch and get them ready for library time," she said. "And thanks again for helping this morning. You basically rescued me."

"It really wasn't anything."

"No, but it was," Jane said, looking him in the eye.

He turned away a little. "Anytime," he said. He waved over his shoulder and slipped out the back door.

Jane gazed after him for a second, thinking about how she could show him her appreciation.

Piper came over and pulled on Jane's hand. "We're hungry," she said.

Jane knelt down. "I know, buddy. How about you guys clean up the golf course and I'll get lunch ready so we can go to story time?"

"Okay," Piper said, skipping off. "You guys, it's time to clean up!"

In the middle of story time, as Jane was sitting in a child-size chair reading *People* magazine, it hit her. She knew exactly how she could help Teo—she would find his dad for him.

She was practically an Internet expert, thanks to all her fandom experience. You learn a lot of tricks about searching when you're desperate for your next fan fiction fix. Particularly when the fan fiction you read is a little off center. She wasn't a SuperWhoLock or something.

Jane wanted to give Teo a hand. It was the least she could do, considering how much he had already helped with the girls—and it was barely two weeks into summer.

This would be a great way to thank him.

Chapter 8

JANE SPENT THE NEXT WEEK TRYING TO FIND HINTS AND clues about Teo's parentage somewhere in the house. She felt weird about snooping, but she told herself she wouldn't dig too deep. She would just look around, superficially.

But after several days of glancing into drawers and peeking in photo albums, she had to give in and take a look through the filing cabinet in the family office in the hope of finding Teo's birth certificate. She needed confirmation of his dad's name. There was no other choice in the matter. She comforted herself with the idea that birth certificates were public record, even though she had no clue whether that was true.

It so happened that on Wednesday afternoon, the twins were out on a playdate and Keegan was playing happily by herself in the basement. Jane took the opportunity as it was presented to her.

She tiptoed into the study under the pretext of running upstairs to get drinks for Keegan and herself. There was a tall filing cabinet in there that Jane hoped would hold the answers she was looking for.

She pulled open the top drawer and was relieved to find that the Garcia-Buchanans were the kind of family who labeled their files. Some of the folders were labeled in Buck's handwriting and some in Connie's. She focused on the latter but still ended up having to go through every drawer to find what she was looking for.

Of course, the drawers were the loudest, squeakiest drawers on earth, and she was already imagining the made-for-TV movie that would be made about her: *Telltale Filing Cabinet: The Jane Connelly Story*. She needed to be quieter or Keegan would come to investigate.

In the bottom drawer she hit the jackpot. There was Teo's birth certificate.

Jose Rodriguez, it read on the line for father's name. Jane wondered for a second whether it was a fake name. She made sure to note the hospital where Teo was born, then slid the drawer closed. She ran back downstairs and was out of breath when she threw herself onto the sectional sofa.

Keegan looked over at her from where she had set up a hair salon for all of the girls' dolls. "Where are our drinks?" she asked.

"Oh, duh," Jane said, still breathless. "I forgot."

"What were you doing up there?"

"I was texting my friend."

"Why were there so many drawers opening and shutting?"

"What are you, a detective?"

Keegan laughed. "No," she said.

"I'll go get us those drinks."

Jane spent the rest of the afternoon trying to search on her phone for information on finding biological parents, but she kept losing the Wi-Fi signal. It didn't help that almost all the information had to do with finding biological parents of people who'd been adopted. Jane wasn't sure whether that information could really help in Teo's situation.

Since Jane wasn't experienced in solving mysteries, she decided the best plan for the evening was to talk to her Magic 8 Ball while streaming multiple episodes of *Veronica Mars*.

"Does Teo's dad want to be found?" she asked the Magic 8.

Don't count on it, it said.

"Hmm," Jane said. "That's not exactly a firm no. I shouldn't count on it, so I won't. What do you think, Veronica?"

Veronica obviously didn't answer, so Jane went back to the Magic 8.

"Can I find Teo's dad?"

Most likely, it said.

"Should I start somewhere besides the Internet?"

It is decidedly so.

"But where?"

The ball couldn't answer questions that didn't have yes-or-no responses, so Jane was left to figure that one out on her own.

She sat down and made a list of who might know anything about Teo's dad.

1. Connie
2. Buck

The list didn't get any longer that night because her favorite *Veronica Mars* episode was up next and Jane decided to give it her full attention.

For research, of course.

The next morning, she didn't wake up thinking about Teo; instead, she woke up with an answer. There was someone who probably knew at least a little more than she did about Teo's dad, and they just so happened to live in the same house. Her mom might be able to help.

It was risky, but potentially worth it in the long run. It was all about taking the right approach and asking the right questions to get the answers she needed.

The problem was that these days any conversation she had with her mother could potentially spiral into yet another argument about college. Jane had gotten really good at avoiding her mother entirely. But an argument with her mom might be worth it to help Teo.

Jane waited for Saturday morning, so she didn't have to run off to babysit. She found her mom in the backyard, pulling weeds from the rock garden.

Jane was about to sit down in one of the patio chairs but then thought better of it. She meandered across the yard and knelt down in the grass next to her mom.

"So which ones are we yanking and which ones are we saving?" Jane asked.

Her mom looked at her doubtfully. "Well, I would highly recommend not yanking the ones with flowers."

"What about this one? This is a weed, right?"

"It is! Good girl," her mom said.

"I'm positive that you're not supposed to talk to your kids like they're dogs."

Her mom smiled and pulled a weed.

Jane pulled a weed, sucked in a deep breath, and dove in. "I've been thinking a lot lately about Connie."

"About what exactly?" Her mom leaned back on her haunches and looked at Jane appraisingly.

"I don't want to be nosy, but I really, really can't help being curious about Teo's dad."

"Oh." Her mom nodded and pursed her lips.

"I guess I wondered if you ever met him."

"Have you talked to Teo about his father?"

"It hasn't come up." Jane licked her lips. "The girls were missing Buck the other day when he was away on business, and I guess it got me thinking about Teo's dad. What happened there?"

"Their lives aren't a soap opera for you to enjoy, Jane."

"Oh, I know. It's just that maybe if I knew a little bit more,

I might know when to tread lightly with certain topics."

"That's very thoughtful of you, Jane," her mom said. "I have to admit I don't know much."

"It's fine, no big deal." But she knew that she'd hit the right tone when her mother continued.

"Connie and I bonded over being pregnant with you and Teo more than anything else. She was wary of telling people too much. I know she was happy that her aunt was so supportive."

"Her aunt?"

"Yeah, don't you remember Connie's aunt Marta? They lived with her until Marta went into assisted living right around the time Connie and Buck got married."

"Is Aunt Marta still alive?"

"Yes. I think they all go to see her at least once a month."

"But that's Connie's aunt? Not anyone from Teo's dad's side of the family?"

"No, I don't know of anyone from Teo's dad's side. Really, Janie, this isn't something Connie and I talked about much. She didn't want anything to do with him for whatever reason." Her mom started digging into the bed with more vigor.

"Yeah, I guess."

"I do understand your curiosity," she said, glancing at Jane.

"You do?"

Her mom shrugged. "Of course. When you start to spend time with a family like that on a daily basis, you learn a lot about them—more than you would have otherwise."

Jane nodded, relief flooding through her. Now she just had to make her getaway, and she could chalk this whole conversation up to a success. The end was in sight.

"Thanks, Mom. Now I feel like I won't blurt out the wrong question at the wrong moment." Jane had already stood up when her mother turned to look at her, shading her eyes from the sun.

"I do feel like I have to point something out."

"What?" Jane asked, even though she *knew* it was a trick.

"Connie hasn't had it easy. Do you remember when you were little and Teo would come over in the evenings while Connie finished her undergrad degree?"

"Maybe?" Jane said. "I'm not sure."

"She's worked very hard. She's really a role model."

"She is," Jane agreed, looking longingly toward the house, hopeful that if she played along for one more second, she could make her escape.

"And maybe you need to keep her in mind when making your own decisions."

Jane huffed out a frustrated breath.

"I'm serious, Janie. Don't put off your education. Do you really want to have to go to college the way Connie did? At night, after work?"

"But I don't even know if a traditional four-year college is really for me," Jane said quietly.

"It's for everyone," her mother said, standing up and wiping her brow with the back of her wrist. "You have absolutely no reason not to go, and I don't understand why you're so stubborn about it."

"Maybe if you let me explain," Jane said.

Her mother crossed her arms. "Explain."

But this wasn't right. This wasn't the moment. Jane didn't have any of her ideas laid out in her head. She had only prepared for the first part of the conversation, not the inevitable second part.

She should have a PowerPoint presentation and index cards. That would be a way to get her mom's attention. Then she might see that while Jane didn't want to go to college, at least she had a plan.

"Not right this second."

"When, Jane? Every time this comes up, you act like you have something better to do. You run away and hide in your room. Isn't it time to face this topic?"

"Why can't we ever talk about something else?"

"Because you need to make some decisions," her mother said, her voice rising to a volume that scared a nearby squirrel.

"It's too hard."

"What is too hard?" Her mother's eyes were steely, and Jane knew there was nothing she could say at this point that would make her mother listen.

"It's too hard to explain it right now."

Her mother's expression said, *I told you so.*

Jane wiped her hands on her shorts. "I do have a plan. It's just not ready yet."

"Well, I'll be waiting to hear all about it."

Jane walked away, hating the way her mother had spoken to her, like she was a child and they were discussing Jane's letter to Santa. Next time she would be ready.

Chapter 9

THE FOURTH OF JULY WAS ONE OF JANE'S FAVORITE HOLIDAYS. There was a huge all-day block party on her street, and then the neighbors would watch the fireworks together at the pool. But this year was a little disappointing.

Jane was at a weird, in-between age. She was too old to participate in the little-kid games, but she hadn't made any plans outside the neighborhood, not having realized that all the kids her age had other things to do, like barbecues with friends or a day at the beach. Margo was one of those people who had plans with friends. She'd invited Jane to go with her, but Jane didn't feel much like tagging along.

She perked up a bit when she ran into Connie as they were setting out the food at the block party.

"Hello, Jane! Gorgeous day," Connie said.

Jane nodded in agreement. "Is Teo going to make an appearance?" She did her best to sound casual, but Teo's presence could definitely turn the day around for her.

"Oh, he had to work. But he should be home later. The pool closes around five or six so they can get ready for the fireworks."

Jane felt her hopes of a fun Fourth of July deflate.

Hours later she sat at a picnic table by herself, consuming a large plate of chocolate chip cookies and contemplating her next fan fiction plot. It might involve Eleven taking Veronica Mars back to 1776 for some convoluted mystery solving. She just needed to figure out why the Doctor would care about American history, being British and all. But she wouldn't know until she tried.

Testing out that plot sounded better than hanging out at the block party for even one more minute. She polished off the last cookie and was about to stand up when Teo straddled the bench next to her.

"Hey," he said.

"Hey," she said, brushing crumbs off her shirt and praying that she didn't have chocolate on her mouth. "I thought you weren't going to be home until six."

"Checking up on me?" he asked.

"For sure. I want to make sure you don't drown."

"I appreciate your concern."

"Oh for the love of—here comes your shadow," Jane said.

"Who? Keegan?" Teo asked, turning to look in the wrong direction.

"No, the other one."

Teo lit up as soon as he saw Ravi. He jumped up and practically hugged him.

"Well, if it isn't my old pal Jane Connelly," Ravi said as he took the seat across from Jane and dragged Teo down next to him. In an ideal world, Teo would have fought Ravi's pull and sat back down next to Jane. "She who kicked me out of my best friend's house."

Jane sat up straight and looked Ravi in the eye. "I'm not going to apologize. You were making me uncomfortable in my place of employment."

Ravi placed both his hands palms down on the tabletop. "Then I have some very good news for Jane." He looked at Teo sadly. "And some bad news for you. My grandma's sick, and I, being the exemplary son that I am, will be traveling to Sri Lanka as my mother's companion. Because obviously she can't function without me."

Jane rolled her eyes. On the one hand, she felt bad for his grandmother. But on the other hand, she'd met Ravi's mother, and Jane was pretty sure it was Ravi who couldn't function without his mom, not the other way around.

"When do you leave?" Teo asked.

"In about an hour," Ravi said, looking at his phone. "In fact, I gotta get out of here. My mom just texted me, like, eighteen times, but I knew I had to say good-bye to you in person, even if it meant having to see Jane the Pain before I left."

"'Jane the Pain'? I feel like you're slipping," Jane said.

"I'll work on it and get back to you," Ravi said, standing up, and this time he and Teo did hug. And then he was gone.

"I know you're not going to understand this, but I'm really going to miss him."

Jane looked over at Teo, shocked. "Of course I get it. My best friends are off at sleepaway band camp for the summer, where there's no cell service and the Wi-Fi signal is on serious lockdown, while I spend my days regretting that I quit playing the glockenspiel in fifth grade."

"So you do get it," Teo said.

"At least we have each other," Jane said, taking a calculated risk.

It paid off when Teo smiled so broadly his dimple made an appearance.

Jane sat on her hands so she wouldn't push her finger into it—that was how adorable his dimple was. She could barely resist the urge to touch it.

"So did you save me any cookies?" Teo asked, gesturing to the empty plate in front of her.

"No," Jane said seriously. "But I did hear that your mom made you a plate of leftovers and put it in the fridge."

"My fridge?"

"That's the rumor."

"Want to come watch me eat?"

"Only if I can bring more cookies."

"What about brownies?" Teo asked, looking over at the dessert table. "Or maybe that apple pie no one has even touched yet."

"It's hard to say no to pie," Jane said.

They stood up and walked over to take the pie.

"Wait," Teo said, grabbing Jane's arm. "Is there ice cream available for the pie?"

"I don't think so. Ice cream doesn't really go with this amount of heat," Jane said.

"Ah, take the pie anyway. I think we have ice cream at my house."

Jane grabbed the pie, and Teo walked in front of her like a bodyguard until they were around the corner and safely inside his house.

He held up his hand to high-five Jane, but she got so flustered she fist-bumped it.

"That's an interesting option." Teo looked at his hand where Jane had basically just punched him.

"I hate myself sometimes," she said.

"Do over?" Teo offered.

"Do over." Jane held up her hand, and this time Teo fist-bumped her palm.

"Thanks for that," she said.

He winked dramatically and then went to rummage in the fridge.

"She took a lot of food for me," Teo said, surveying the plate that was piled high with various salads and three different kinds of meat.

"I think she might be trying to fatten you up."

He patted his abs. "Probably."

After about an hour of eating the block-party leftovers and more than their fair share of pie, Jane and Teo decided it was probably time to rejoin their neighbors.

"Are you going to the fireworks?" Teo asked as they exited his house.

"Honestly? I'm tired of basically everyone. I think I've had enough togetherness for one day. I had been planning to go inside and watch the Macy's fireworks on TV."

"Are you tired of me, too?" Teo asked, raising an eyebrow and looking at Jane from the corner of his eye.

"Well, no. You don't count."

"Then what if we watched them from your roof? I bet we'd have a sweet view from up there."

Jane glanced at her roof and then back at Teo.

"Seriously?"

"Sure. I don't really feel like going down with my family, but I don't really feel like sitting around by myself, either."

"Especially with your shadow Ravi out of the country," Jane said, a teasing lilt to her voice.

"Exactly," Teo said, playing along.

When their parents left for the fireworks, Teo begged off by saying he was tired, and Jane said she would keep him company. It was that easy.

"Now we just have to get onto the roof without killing ourselves, and we're golden," Jane said as they walked up her front steps.

"Jane, even if you fell, there's no way you would die. You might break your legs, but you would survive."

"Not helping," Jane said.

"Your house is exactly the same," Teo said as they entered her front door.

"My parents painted. And put in new carpeting."

Teo shrugged. "It looks nice. I like it more than what my mom and Buck did to our house," he muttered as they walked up the stairs. Jane mentally took stock of how her bedroom looked at that moment and hoped that she'd at least made her bed that morning.

"I think your house looks awesome. Like something from a magazine."

"Yeah, but is that really a good thing? It has no character. It's cookie cutter."

Jane giggled. "I think you've been watching too many episodes of *House Hunters*."

"Maybe I have," he said with a grin.

She peeked into her room before letting Teo in and let out a sigh of relief when she realized it wasn't a total disaster.

"How are things with Buck?" Jane asked as they climbed out her bedroom window and then settled on the roof with their backs against a dormer.

"What do you mean?" Teo asked, tensing up a little.

"I don't know. It's weird because you guys seem to get along, but sometimes he's like . . ." Jane paused, searching for the right word. "Just trying way too hard. Like a brand-new teacher who's just got out of college and wants to talk about how he was a big football hero a couple years ago."

Teo threw his head back and laughed. "Wow. You totally nailed it. He's really weird around me, right?"

"Oh, totally. I think he really wants to be bros with you."

"Gross. I don't want to be bros with Buck."

"But think about it. Like, when he tries to talk to you about baseball or lifting weights. Or the other morning when he tried to bond with you over the supermodel on the *Today* show."

"You're so right. I never put it into those words before, but that's totally it."

"I'm intimately familiar with awkward family dynamics."

"You, with the two parents and the sister and the actual white picket fence?" Teo asked.

"Well, that's from the outside. The inside is a whole other story."

"What kind of story?"

"I don't know. You'll think it's weird," Jane said quietly.

"Oh come on, you totally called the Buck thing. You might as well share your family crap."

"I don't know. It sucks being the idiot in a family of geniuses."

Teo looked less surprised than Jane would have liked.

"Yeah, I get that, too."

"Keegan and the twins are in Mensa?"

"No. I don't mean the genius thing. I mean, like, um . . ." He shook his head and looked at the sky, and Jane had the keen feeling that Teo wasn't going to say much more that night about anything of importance. And she wouldn't push him.

"Ah, you know. The stepfather crap. Them being my half sisters," Teo said, waving a hand as if to clear the air. "But your family aren't all geniuses. I mean, they're nice people, but they're normal smart. You're just smart in a different way."

Jane accepted the subject change. "I'm average at best. And they're all like—"

The boom of the first firework swallowed up the rest of her sentence.

"To be continued," Jane said. Teo smiled.

Teo lay back on the roof with his arms under his head, and Jane mirrored him.

"This would be extremely romantic with the right person," Jane said.

"And I'm the wrong person?" Teo asked with a devilish grin.

"What? No! I didn't mean it like that. I just meant . . . Well, I didn't even really mean to say it out loud."

Teo nodded.

"I'm a freaking mess sometimes."

"Aren't we all," Teo said.

Jane closed her eyes and imagined what a different kind of girl would do in this moment, the kind of girl who was confident and didn't feel the need to consult a fortune-telling toy before making any decisions. She let out a deep breath and opened her eyes to find Teo watching her.

He grinned sheepishly.

Grins like that should be illegal, Jane thought.

They sat quietly for a moment after the show ended. Everything seemed darker than before the fireworks started, like there wasn't any light in the whole world.

"Guess I'd better go," he said, slipping back through the window. He extended his hand to help Jane through.

It was sweaty and made Jane feel better about not being the only nervous one.

Or maybe her hand was sweaty.

It was hard to tell, so she pulled away fast and rubbed her hand on her shorts.

They stood in the middle of her room, and the bed seemed to loom large in front of them, making Jane have thoughts suited more to fan fiction than to real life.

She shook her head, trying to clear away the weird thoughts that seemed so loud she wouldn't be shocked if Teo could hear them.

"Well," he said.

"Well," Jane said, nodding.

Teo took a deep breath, opening his mouth like he was about to say something important and memorable, something that might change the course of everything.

Instead, he hooked a thumb toward the bedroom door and left without another word.

Jane peeked out the window and watched him walk home.

He glanced up and caught her there, peering out at him, and he waved.

Normally she would have been embarrassed, but right now she was happy that he was the kind of guy who looked back one more time.

Chapter 10

ON THE FIFTH OF JULY, MARGO WAS UP EARLY, WAITING FOR her sister to emerge from her bedroom cocoon so Margo could ask her a favor. By nine a.m. Margo was getting antsy. By ten she couldn't sit still.

"Margo, are you having some kind of episode?" her father asked.

"I wanted to ask Jane something," she said innocently.

"Why don't you go wake her up instead of flitting around here like some kind of possessed hummingbird?"

Using her father's words as permission, Margo flew up the stairs and knocked on Jane's door until she finally heard a muffled "Come in."

"Janie," Margo said.

"Margo, I'm busy," Jane said, rolling onto her stomach

and pulling her covers over her head.

"Jane," Margo whined.

"No."

"You don't even know what I was going to ask."

Jane huffed and flipped over. "What? What do you need from me?"

"You have a pool pass, right?"

"Yeah, Connie bought it for me," Jane said, leaning on her elbows.

"Can you bring guests in?"

"Yes. A day pass is, like, five dollars."

"Can you bring me in?"

"Why do you want to go to the pool?"

"I don't know—it's something different to do."

"We could go to the beach," Jane offered.

"No way," Margo said. "It's Fourth of July weekend. The place is crawling with Bennies."

"Good point. Let's avoid the out-of-towners," Jane said, lying back on her pillows and yawning.

"It'll be fun," Margo said.

"Yeah, I'm not so sure about that."

"Maybe Teo will be working."

Jane sat up straight and narrowed her eyes at her sister.

"I mean, because you guys are becoming friends, not for any other reason," Margo added, wanting to hedge her bets. Even though she was sure that Jane was nursing a big old crush on Teo, she didn't want to freak her out about it. And she didn't want Jane to say no to taking her to the pool.

Jane chewed her lip for a second. "Fine. We'll go. But I need food first."

"I'll buy you a bacon-egg-and-cheese bagel."

Jane hopped out of the bed and patted her sister's head. "You've won me over with your generous spirit."

"Awesome," Margo said. Since Jane seemed so pleased, Margo didn't mention that the bagel would cost her all of two dollars.

"I'll drive," she offered when they were outside.

"No way. I want to drive," Jane said, snatching the keys out of her sister's hand and racing for the car. Margo had to admit it was nice to let someone else drive for a change.

It was the kind of day where the sun didn't just beat down on the cracked pavement—it pulsed. Ordinarily, the pool would be packed from one end to the other. But since it was Fourth of July weekend, people had other things to do.

After eating their bagels while lounging on the lawn surrounding the pool, they walked through the gates and were surveying their available options when someone spoke up behind them.

"If I'd known you'd be making an appearance, I would have reserved the VIP area."

Margo hadn't seen Jane look so happy since the Christmas when she was ten and her parents had bought her a lime-green mountain bike.

"Hey," Jane said.

"Hey," Teo replied.

And then they just stood there looking at each other idiotically for what felt like a thousand years.

"Hi!" Margo finally said, leaning into Teo's line of sight.

"Hey, Margo. I didn't even see you there."

"Thanks," she said.

He didn't even register Margo's sarcasm before turning back to Jane.

"Last night was fun," he said.

"It was," Jane agreed.

Then a whistle blew from across the pool and Teo had to rush away, but Margo already had plenty of ammunition for torturing her sister all afternoon.

"We have a great view of the lifeguards," Margo said as they dropped their stuff onto deck chairs at the far end of the pool.

"Why would I want a great view of the lifeguards?" Jane asked.

Margo looked at Jane pointedly.

"We're just friends," Jane said, but her blush gave her away.

"I don't believe you."

"I swear!"

"Tell me what happened last night, and I'll tell you whether you're 'just friends,'" Margo said as they slipped into the pool.

Jane dragged out the story of watching the fireworks with Teo on the roof far longer than was really necessary while they bobbed in the deep end, but by the time she finished, it was obvious that Jane had a whopper of a crush on their neighbor. It almost made Margo not want to tease her too much.

Almost.

When they were getting out of the pool, an Asian girl who was vaguely familiar to Margo approached them.

"Hey," Jane said to the girl. Then she turned to Margo. "This is Claudia Lee."

"Oh, hey," Margo said.

"And this is my sister, Margo," Jane said to Claudia.

"Hey," Claudia said. "I think we were in the same art class my freshman year."

"Yeah, totally," Margo said. "I knew you looked familiar."

Jane's jaw dropped. "You took art class?" she asked her sister.

"Yeah. I had a spot for an elective my junior year, and it seemed like a fun one."

Margo didn't mention that she actually transferred into it to hang out with a girl named Kara Maxwell. She also didn't mention that while she was out with her friends yesterday, she learned that the very same Kara Maxwell was an assistant manager at the pool. Margo kept both of those facts to herself.

"What are you doing here?" Jane asked, taking her seat and motioning for Claudia to take the one next to her.

"The usual," Claudia said, gesturing toward a group of kids.

"Claudia is in charge of her stepbrother and stepsister every freaking day of her life," Jane informed Margo, who nodded and slid her sunglasses back up her nose to hide her eyes.

Kara Maxwell had finally taken the lifeguard stand.

While Jane and Claudia chatted like old friends, Margo spent the next few hours watching Kara rotate around the pool from one lifeguard chair to the next while trying to think of a decent opening line.

They hadn't exactly been close in high school. Margo had only watched Kara from afar, but maybe that could change now.

Margo was pleased when Teo went back on rotation. She liked the idea that she wasn't the only person sitting there pining for one of the lifeguards.

"You got it bad for him," Claudia said, looking up from her book to follow Jane's line of sight.

"I do not."

Margo leaned over to address Claudia. "She totally does. And he's definitely into her, too. You should have seen them trying to flirt earlier."

"Don't worry," Claudia said. "I get to witness it every day at swim class."

"Do we really have to discuss this in earshot of him?" Jane asked, casting a desperate glance in Teo's direction.

"Something happened last night," Margo told Claudia, pitching her voice a little lower.

Claudia punched Jane in the arm. "Why didn't you tell me?"

"We just watched the fireworks together! We're friends. I don't *like*-like him."

Margo smirked and Claudia raised a doubtful eyebrow.

"Fine. Whatever. I appreciate him—"

"You appreciate his buttocks," Claudia interrupted.

"I appreciate him," Jane continued, undeterred, "for being helpful and sweet."

"You love him," Margo said.

"No, no," Claudia said. "She doesn't love him, but she definitely *lurves* him."

"A very important distinction," Margo said.

"What's the opposite of lurve?" Jane asked. "Because that's how I feel about the two of you."

"Ouch. Burn," Claudia said. "So if you guys aren't here to check out Teo, and you're not here because of babysitting, then why are you here?"

Jane looked at Margo. "It was her idea."

"Margo, you really couldn't think of anything better to do?"

Margo shook her head sadly. "You were in art with me. You know I'm not that creative."

"Oh, oh," Claudia whispered, patting Jane's arm to get her attention and tipping her chin in the other direction. "Teo."

Jane sat up straighter and tried to fix her hair a bit, even though there really wasn't any hope, between the chlorine and the sun drying it out.

But it was the attempt that solidified for Margo that Jane had it bad for this kid.

"Hey," Teo said.

"Hi," Jane said, her voice breathy.

Margo mouthed *Just act normal!* at Jane, who tried to smile but looked more like she was about to have oral surgery than like she was happy to see Teo.

Margo tried to think of something else to say to fill the silence and to cover up for Jane who was quietly freaking out for no apparent reason. Then she caught sight of someone else approaching them.

Kara Maxwell.

Margo pulled her towel up higher out of fear of a nip slip and pushed her sunglasses up on her head, hoping to miraculously tame her own hair.

"Hey, Margo!" Kara said.

Margo sighed with relief at Kara's apparent enthusiasm, but the sigh got mixed in with her greeting and she ended up sounding nearly as breathy as Jane had.

"I was coming over to see if you guys were giving Teo a hard time, but I guess not." Kara glanced at the other two girls and nodded in greeting.

Kara looked over at Claudia. "Hey, what's up? I was just texting your brother. I hear you guys are having your annual Uncle Bru party soon."

"We are," Claudia said. "You guys should all come, too."

"Um, okay," Jane said.

"All of you," Claudia said, looking at Teo and Margo.

"Sounds fun," Teo said, glancing over at Jane, only to catch Jane looking up at him. They both looked away bashfully.

"My brother, Darryl, and I have a party at our uncle's place every summer. He goes on some kind of fishing trip with his college buddies. I'll never understand how he doesn't notice. But I guess it's kind of a don't ask, don't tell thing."

Margo could have sworn that Kara looked over at her for a split second as though Margo would understand the "don't ask, don't tell" reference better than anyone else in the group. It gave her the smallest shred of hope.

Because Margo actually had no clue whether Kara was into girls. Margo had heard some things, but she didn't know for sure.

Margo stood up quickly, surprising everyone.

"We should exchange numbers," she said to Kara, waving her phone around.

"Sure," Kara said. "I'll give you mine, and you should text me."

"So when is this blowout going on?" Margo asked Claudia.

"Next Saturday," Claudia said. "I'll shoot Jane the details."

The five of them talked for a few more minutes, and then Teo and Kara left to do their next rotation and Jane mumbled something about wanting to go.

Things couldn't have gone better for Margo, so she didn't mind leaving. In fact, it was probably the best day Margo had had all summer. Maybe even all year.

"You can drive home," Jane said, tossing her the keys on the way to the car.

Margo pulled out of the pool parking, and Jane's hand slapped against the dash as she braced herself.

"Oh my God, Margo! Didn't you see that minivan?" Jane asked.

"What? No. I must have missed it."

Jane was quiet for a moment. "I didn't know you knew Kara Maxwell."

"Um. Yeah. We went to high school together, but we were never close."

"It's so nice to see you making friends after all these years, Margo," Jane said in a fairly good impression of their mother.

"Like you were making friends with Teo, hmm? That kind of friend?"

Jane opened her mouth to respond, then covered her eyes as Margo nearly clipped a pedestrian.

"Sorry!" Margo shouted out the window.

"You're a really bad driver."

"I'm offensive as opposed to defensive," Margo said.

"If you say so," Jane said.

"There are all different kinds of drivers."

"Uh-huh. And, for the record, Teo and I really are just friends."

"Just friends *for now*," Margo said. "What you need is a plan."

Jane rolled her eyes.

Margo smiled. "Do you want ice cream? I'm in the mood for ice cream."

Jane white-knuckled the door handle as Margo U-turned across a four-lane road to get a parking spot.

"I would love ice cream, but I'm totally driving home. My heart can't take this," Jane said as they got out of the car.

"You sound like Mom."

"That's a terrible thing to say!" Jane said, passing her sister and running for the door of the ice-cream shop. "Oh, and you're paying or else I'll tell Mom you tried to kill a pedestrian."

"She'll never believe you."

"I can be fairly persuasive."

It was Margo's turn to roll her eyes, but she paid for the ice cream, just in case.

Chapter 11

THE WEEK AFTER THE HOLIDAY DRAGGED FOR JANE. SHE SAW Teo only a couple of times, but each time he mentioned the upcoming party. So that was good news.

On Friday afternoon as she was leaving work, Jane got up the courage to ask him if he wanted to go to the party with her and Margo.

"Oh, I'm actually going with some of the other lifeguards right from the pool, but I'll see you there," he said.

Jane searched his face in the hope of detecting some disappointment, but she didn't find any.

On Saturday night, she and Margo managed to get out of the house without too much fuss.

"I think they're really excited that we're hanging out together," Margo said as they walked to the car. Their parents had even extended Jane's curfew until twelve thirty.

"I have to agree," Jane said as she walked right to the driver's side.

"I could drive."

"You are the worst driver on earth, and I want to actually make it to this party alive."

Margo slouched in the passenger seat and crossed her arms. "Fine."

They parked a couple of blocks away from Claudia's uncle's house, just as Claudia had instructed. When they got to the house, there was a message written in sidewalk chalk on the driveway: SHUT UP AND WALK AROUND BACK! it said.

When they got to the backyard, there was a huge deck and a view of the ocean.

Jane definitely understood why Claudia and her brother had a party there every summer.

"Won't the neighbors complain about the noise?" Jane asked.

Margo shrugged. "It's not really that loud. And at least some of the noise is drowned out by the ocean."

Jane and Margo went inside to see who was around, said hi to Claudia and Darryl, and then went back outside to get drinks.

"I won't drink," Jane said. "I'll drive home."

"You're just terrified of my driving."

"There's that, but I also don't really care about drinking."

"Have you ever gotten drunk?" Margo asked.

"No, and I really don't think tonight's the night to start."

"Start what?" a voice asked behind them.

"Oh! Hello, Teo!" Margo said.

"Hey, Margo," he said, obviously confused by her enthusiastic greeting.

"Well, I see someone over there I need to talk to," Margo said, pointing in a vague direction and leaving Teo and Jane standing by the keg.

"Are you drinking?" he asked, starting to pump a cup of beer for himself.

"Um, no. That's what I was saying to Margo. I don't really drink."

"Oh, that's cool. Me neither," he said, taking a sip.

"What do you call that?"

"Drinking. But I mean I don't get drunk. Not really. I have one or two, for the sake of being social."

Jane nodded and peeked into one of the coolers, happy to find a bottle of water.

"This is me being social," she said, taking a sip.

"If anyone asks, tell them it's straight vodka, and they'll think you're a complete badass."

"Oh, I am a complete badass. That's for damn sure."

"No doubt about it."

They stood there looking at each other for a minute before they realized that they were in the way of everyone else trying to get to the keg.

"Let's find somewhere to sit," Teo said.

Jane was surprised that he didn't run back to his friends

right away, but she decided to enjoy being with him while she could.

They found a spot below the deck, where there were a few scattered lawn chairs that no one had claimed yet. Teo got up a few times to fill his cup while they talked, but Jane was thrilled that he kept coming back to her. Before long he was more than a little bit tipsy.

"I'm sorry," he said as he meandered back after his fourth refill, weaving between the chairs. "I should go find my friends. I don't want to monopolize all your time."

"You're not," Jane said, shaking her head. "If I wasn't talking to you, I would be following Margo around."

Teo smiled and plopped back down in the seat Jane had saved for him.

"Unless you want to go find your friends. I know I saw the guys from the soccer team."

"Nah, I think I like it right here with you."

Flattery would get him everywhere with Jane.

By ten o'clock, Teo had moved past tipsy and well into drunk territory.

"So," he said, smiling, looking more than a little loopy but so cute Jane couldn't stop staring at him.

She shook her head.

"What?" he asked.

"I thought you didn't get drunk," Jane teased.

"I'm okay. I'm fine," he said, slurring his words.

"Yeah, you seem fine."

"Look," he said, standing up and handing Jane his beer. He stood on one foot and tried to tap his nose with his fingertip, alternating hands the way cops make drunk drivers do. Except Teo kept completely missing his face.

"I don't think that's working," Jane said.

He giggled and sat back down. "That wasn't working."

Jane laughed.

"Is it hot out?" he asked.

"Yeah, it is."

"Good, I'm glad it's not just me. I think, you know, in, like, Siberia they put whispey, whisquey, whisp—" He blew a raspberry and tried again, laughing at himself. "Whiskey! They put whiskey in, like, those barrels around a dog's neck and then, like, people out in the cold drink the whiskey or something? To get warm?"

"I don't know if they really do that in real life. It might only be for cartoons. But, yes, I know what you're talking about."

"I was worried that beer did the same thing as whiskey, made you really hot."

"It might," Jane said. "I don't know what beer is truly capable of."

"You know, you're smarter than you pretend to be."

"What?" she asked.

"You're smart. Even though you think you're not that smart. But you talk like you're smart."

"I have a decent vocabulary, nothing too flashy. I blame my parents. But being able to *talk* like you're smart and actually *being* smart are really different things."

He dug into his back pocket and pulled out his wallet, handing it to Jane. "Count my money. Please."

"This is very weird."

"Yeah, but I'm drunker than I expected and . . ." He paused, shrugging. "I don't know. I don't remember what I was going to say."

She patted his shoulder and couldn't stop smiling.

"How much money do I have?"

"You have seventeen dollars."

"I bet you seventeen dollars that you're smart."

He took his wallet and put it back in his pocket and then shook Jane's hand.

"All right," she said.

When they were done shaking hands, he leaned his elbows on his knees and stared at the ground. Jane poked his side, and he looked over at her.

"Hi," he said.

"Hi."

"What are we going to do about you?" Teo asked.

"Me?" Jane asked, putting her hand to her chest to feign shock. "What about you? You are one sorry drunk."

"I'm not sorry."

"Fine. But you are drunk."

"How are we going to settle this bet about how smart you are?" he asked.

"I don't know. It's a tough one."

He put his hand out to her, and Jane took it, thinking he wanted to shake again, but instead he held on to it, twining their fingers together.

"I like your nail polish," he said, smoothing his thumb over it.

"It's called Sweet Escape."

"It's the color of a Creamsicle."

"I'm sorry to say it doesn't taste like a Creamsicle." The whole moment was surreal to Jane. It was like she was talking from outside her body. It felt like something was happening around her instead of to her.

"What are you escaping from?"

She didn't answer, instead drawing his hand closer to her and studying it in the light from the deck.

"What are you doing?" he asked, his voice right in her ear, his breath raising the hairs on her neck.

"I'm looking at your palm."

"Are you going to read it?"

"I was thinking about it." She traced the lines on it lightly, and he shivered. Jane glanced over at him. He looked a little lost, but a lot less sleepy all of a sudden.

"I think we're a lot alike, Jane Connelly," he said.

"I think maybe we are, too," she said after a while.

He pulled his hand away and leaned back in his chair, looking at the stars.

"There's a lot of stuff people don't know about," he said.

She watched his eyes dart back and forth, like he was

searching for something up there besides the stars and the low-flying planes.

"I don't know a lot of stuff," he continued. "But I want to learn everything."

Her heart constricted, and she felt tears rise in her eyes. Something about Teo in this moment was everything she loved and hated about life, all rolled into one.

The next thing Jane knew, Teo leaned over in his chair, closed his eyes, and aimed for the approximate location of her lips. But his drunk brain misjudged the distance, and instead he fell out of his chair and flat on his face.

"Ouch," he muttered, rolling over.

Jane could hardly stop laughing. "Are you okay?"

"That was supposed to be romantic," he said mournfully. "Like on the roof. I was going to be the right person."

Jane offered her hand to him. "Come on," she said, helping him sit up.

"That hurt my arm and my pride." He scrunched up his face. "I am really thirsty. I should have more beer." He scrambled to his feet, but Jane pushed him back into his chair.

"No more beer. I'll get you some water."

"Okay, fine," he said, huffing out a breath.

"Stay here," she said. "I'll be back."

He nodded.

Jane went in search of the cooler where she'd found water bottles earlier, but it was empty. She went into the house but couldn't find any cups to get water from the tap, and there was nothing in the refrigerator besides pickles and leftover takeout containers. She saw an open door leading out to the garage, and another fridge out there, along with a gorgeous red convertible. She didn't know much about cars, but this one was so pretty she wanted to take a picture.

She grabbed a couple of bottles of water from the garage fridge, and when she turned around, she heard a rustling noise coming from the car. Then she saw some movement in the dim light. What if it was a murderer?

"Ah! Don't hurt me!" she cried, dropping the bottles. Two human heads popped up. "Shit, sorry. You scared me."

"You think *we* scared *you*," a girl's voice said.

Then a different girl's voice giggled. "Seriously. I thought you closed the door, Margo."

"I thought I did."

"Margo?" Jane asked into the darkness.

"Jane?"

Jane's eyes finally adjusted to the dim light, and there, in the front seat of the convertible, were her sister and Kara Maxwell, their hands still on each other.

Margo slid across the bench seat away from Kara, looking guilty.

Jane picked up the water and walked quickly out of the garage. She heard Margo say, "I'll be back," and then a ruckus as she tried to hop over the car door rather than simply opening it.

"Wait, Jane."

Jane stopped.

"Please. Can we talk?"

Jane turned around.

"Please don't tell Mom and Dad."

Jane laughed. "I promise I have zero interest in talking to Mom and Dad about you making out in a garage with Kara Maxwell."

Margo put her hands over her eyes. "I really didn't want you to find out this way."

"To find out what?"

"That I'm bi, obviously."

Jane's jaw dropped. She hadn't even considered the implications. Finding your sister making out with anyone is weird.

"Considering it happened like seven seconds ago, I haven't really had time to process the details," Jane said.

"Are you mad?" Margo asked.

"Of course I'm not mad. It was unexpected. But not anything worth getting mad about."

Margo crossed her arms, like she was trying to give herself a hug. "What do you think Mom and Dad are going to say?"

"Margo, seriously, it's been all of twenty seconds now. It's a lot to process, even without all these questions."

"You're mad."

Jane rolled her eyes and shifted the bottles of water over to one arm. She pulled her sister into a hug with the other.

"I'm not mad. That would be the stupidest thing ever to be mad about."

Margo sighed with relief.

"Now, come on, Teo is basically shit-faced, and I need to get this water back to him. And we should probably go home, since it's almost midnight."

"Time flies," Margo said. "Let me go say good-bye to Kara, and I'll meet you at the car."

Jane collected Teo, and they made their way to the car. Margo was already waiting there.

"You okay, Teo?" Margo asked as they approached.

He nodded, and Jane opened the back door for him.

"Thanks, you guys," Teo said as he threw himself into the backseat.

"Please don't vomit in my car," Margo said.

"Please don't vomit in *my* car," Jane said, looking at Margo pointedly.

"Please stop talking about vomit," Teo said.

Chapter 12

THE KNOCK ON TEO'S DOOR ON SUNDAY MORNING WAS definitely not a quiet one. It was a knock to wake the dead, and it carried on for what felt like hours, until Teo's groggy brain allowed him to move enough to stumble out of bed. He shed his tangled sheets and barely remained upright, but he managed to lurch over to the door to stop the god-awful racket.

Before he opened the door, he took stock. All he could really feel was an epic thirst. It was like his whole body was thirsty. His eyes, his skin, his hair—it was all thirsty. Not just his mouth.

As he opened the door, he prayed silently that it wouldn't be Buck. Anyone but Buck. Teo couldn't handle his stepfather at the moment. But of course it was Buck on the other side, holding up Teo's cell phone. Because that was how life worked.

"This has been in the living room making noise for the past two hours," Buck said.

"I'm sorry," Teo said, taking it from him.

It was only 7:02 in the morning. No wonder Teo was exhausted. And no wonder his cell phone was making a lot of noise. He had about fifty notifications ranging from texts making sure he got home okay to photos that he'd been tagged in to new friend requests.

"Why have you been in the living room since five?" Teo asked, rubbing at his eyes.

Buck rubbed his own tired eyes. "Keegan had a nightmare. She went back to sleep, but I couldn't."

Teo yawned and leaned on the doorjamb. "Oh God, that sucks," he said.

Buck nodded.

Teo wasn't going to remain upright much longer. "Anything else?" he asked, hoping to cut through Buck's usual hemming and hawing.

"Yeah, the lawn," Buck said. "It needs to be mowed."

"Right this minute?"

"No, but sooner rather than later. Definitely today."

"But I just did it," Teo said, the whine in his voice making a headache spike behind his eyes.

"The grass continues to grow, Teo," Buck said with the barest edge of impatience in his voice. "And I know you missed curfew last night."

Now Teo understood. "Are you going to tell my mom?"

"I should, but I won't if you do the lawn today."

"I can do that. I have today off. Any chance I could go back to sleep for a little bit?"

"Yeah, sure," Buck said, patting him awkwardly on the shoulder before turning to go downstairs. "Make sure you shower, too. You smell like a distillery."

Teo sniffed at his shirt but couldn't really smell anything.

After brushing his teeth and drinking vast quantities of water from the bathroom sink, Teo threw himself back into bed and fell into a fitful sleep.

The alcohol had made his brain a little foggy, but when he woke up next, he felt a lot better. His conversation with Buck seemed like a dream.

Teo tried to put the pieces of last night back together, and a lot of it featured Jane. He opened the notifications on his phone and found that all the pictures he was tagged in also featured Jane.

Jane and him by the keg.

Jane and him in the background talking.

Jane and him sitting in lawn chairs, looking at the sky.

The evening definitely had a theme. Teo stared at the images, trying to remember what they had talked about, but he really wasn't sure. It made him nervous not to know.

Teo had a tendency to latch onto people. There weren't a lot of people who appreciated that quality. Hopefully, Jane didn't mind.

He sat straight up in bed, a cry of horror on his lips.

He had tried to kiss Jane and failed spectacularly.

He exhaled through his nose and tried to remember the lead-up to the kiss. Maybe she had wanted to kiss; maybe he'd been reading the signs better because he was some kind of drunken kissing savant.

The smell of pancakes drifted upstairs, and Teo decided it was time to get out of bed and face Buck. And the lawn. And his newfound feelings for Jane that he hadn't even known about until he got drunk last night.

He got out of bed and showered fast, keeping the water on the cold side to wake up his fuzzy brain.

Buck was cooking at the stove and Teo's sisters were all sitting around the table when he walked into the kitchen. They greeted him with their usual exuberance.

"Teo!" Keegan said, her voice like knives stabbing at his mushy skull. If this was what a hangover felt like, Teo's drinking days would be over before they even really got started.

Piper and Rory acted like they hadn't seen him in months, even though he'd had dinner with them last night.

"Mommy's taking us to see Tía Marta today," Rory said.

"Sounds fun," Teo walked over to Buck to get a plate of food for himself. Buck piled a plate high with pancakes and then sort of leered at Teo, as if daring him to consume so much breakfast after he'd been drinking. But the joke was on Buck because Teo was more than up to the challenge. It wasn't his stomach that was bothering him.

"Are you going to come with us?" Piper asked. How had he never noticed that her voice was like nails on a chalkboard?

"No," Teo said, glancing over at Buck and doing his best to keep from sounding too whiny. "I need to stay home and mow the lawn."

"Boo, that's boring," Keegan said.

"I know. But it'll make the house look nice," Teo said.

The girls seemed less than impressed.

Teo's mom swept into the room then, kissed all the girls on top of their heads, and then stopped when she got to Teo.

"Are you ill?" she asked, putting her hand on his forehead.

"No, no. I slept like crap last night." He stopped himself before he said anything further, not wanting to raise his mother's suspicions.

As a kid, this exchange would have taken place in Spanish. Teo missed those days; it was like they shared a secret language back then, even though Spanish wasn't actually a secret and millions of people all over the world spoke it.

Not to mention that he was getting pretty rusty at the language and found it harder and harder to translate his thoughts. But he still missed that closeness with his mom.

She took a plate of food from Buck and kissed his cheek. "This looks delicious," she said, sitting down at the table. "Why didn't you sleep well, Teo?" she asked.

Again, he took a quick glance at Buck, who wasn't paying any attention but instead was washing the pans in the sink and whistling.

"I guess I have a lot on my mind. Thinking about college and stuff."

His mother nodded. "Are you narrowing down your list?"

"Yeah. I'm getting closer. I'll be ready to apply after I take the SATs again in October."

"Good boy. Are you coming with us to see Tía Marta?"

"I promised Buck I'd mow the lawn."

His mom smiled and patted his hand. "Thank you. We appreciate it."

They finished up breakfast after that, and his mom and sisters left while Buck went into the study to pay some bills. Teo was certain he was actually updating his fantasy baseball league, but he was in no position to call Buck out on something like that today.

Teo was still thirsty, but working out in the sun actually felt really good, like he was sweating the last of the alcohol out of his system. Buck had definitely underestimated the metabolism of a seventeen-year-old boy.

He weighed the pros and cons of walking over to Jane's house and seeing how she reacted to him. Maybe she'd been really drunk last night, too. Although he kind of remembered her driving home, so probably not. Which meant she would remember every humiliating moment of his literal nosedive.

"How's it going?" Buck asked when Teo went into the house to get more water after working for a couple of hours.

"It's hot as balls."

"Are you done?" Buck asked, ignoring Teo's complaint.

"Almost," Teo said, scrolling through his phone. Ravi had e-mailed him four times in the past hour. Apparently, he really wanted to Skype with Teo immediately.

Teo shot back a quick e-mail that he would sign on to Skype in an hour, after he finished being Buck's landscaper.

It had been only a little over a week since Ravi left, but Teo had no clue what they were going to talk about once they got past the initial catch-up. Maybe Ravi would have a lot to say about his grandmother's health and his family in Sri Lanka. Teo certainly wasn't going to bring up whatever was going on with Jane. Not only because he had no clue how to classify it—because, oh God, he had definitely tried to kiss her—but also because he wasn't interested in another long lecture about "bros before hos."

Jane was not a ho.

But Ravi was still his bro.

It was a lot for Teo to make sense of on a good day, and he definitely wasn't firing on all cylinders.

Buck was nowhere to be found when Teo finished up outside. He got himself another gigantic glass of water and then went up to his room to log on to Skype.

He sent Ravi a message to tell him he was online, and soon enough they were chatting. Usually they would text, but today Ravi wanted to video chat so he could keep playing some game on his DS.

"So what's up? What am I missing?" Ravi asked, not looking at Teo.

"I went to a party at Claudia Lee's uncle's house last night," Teo said, leaning back in his computer chair and yawning.

"Yeah, I saw something about that online," Ravi said in an offhand way that Teo could tell was actually masking jealousy.

"It was fun."

"Who'd you go with?"

"Work people. They all know her brother. That's kind of how I got invited."

"Sounds better than what I did last night."

Teo prepared himself for the onslaught of Ravi's "oh, woe is me" rant. Teo knew Ravi deserved to rant. A sick grandma totally gave him the right. But the problem with Ravi was that he was kind of the Boy Who Cried Woe Is Me. With him, everything tended to be dramatic and terrible, even when things weren't really that bad.

"What did you do?"

"Played some kind of Sri Lankan board game with my cousins and went to bed at a reasonable hour. What time is it at home? I think I've totally lost touch with eastern standard time."

"It's almost noon."

"I can't wait to come home."

"When do you think that'll be?"

Ravi shrugged. "My grandma's going to be fine, but it's like now that we're here, my mom doesn't want to leave right away. And she wants to stay for at least two weeks after my grandma gets out of the hospital, to make sure she's okay at home."

"Sucks."

"What's up with you?" Ravi asked.

"Buck is being kind of an ass about the lawn thing again. We go around in circles about it every summer. He acts like I'm always trying to get out of it, even though I've never once tried to." Looking at Ravi on-screen, Teo knew his friend wasn't paying any attention to the conversation, and Teo had no idea how to make him. He couldn't exactly reach through the screen and punch him, like he normally would in this situation.

"Do you want to go?" Teo asked.

"What? No. Go on. Buck's treating you like the landscaper again. I know how it is."

Teo rolled his eyes, but he still didn't feel like he was really being heard.

When Ravi ended the call because it was getting late in Sri Lanka, Teo idly Googled his dad's name for a little while before going back downstairs when he heard his mom and sisters get home.

"The yard looks really good, Teo," Buck said while they were watching the Phillies game later that night. The girls were already in bed, and Teo's mom was working away on her laptop in the kitchen. "You obviously worked really hard on it."

Teo was so taken aback that he couldn't speak for a moment.

"Thanks, Buck," he finally said. "I didn't think you ever really noticed."

"You're welcome," Buck said. And then he smirked. "Maybe you should always mow the lawn hung over."

"I wasn't—" Teo started to say.

Buck held up his hand. "No judgment."

In what Teo considered a moment of growth, he decided to walk away before either he or Buck ruined the best conversation they'd ever had.

Chapter 13

JANE HAD SPENT THE VAST MAJORITY OF SUNDAY MORNING bouncing from room to room, trying to find the best vantage point to watch Teo mow his lawn. As creepy as it was, she couldn't bring herself to stop. He was very pretty out there in the sun, getting sweaty, taking off his shirt. He was like a guy in a deodorant commercial.

She could only get a good look at him when he was working in the backyard, because of how the houses were laid out, but lucky for Jane, the Buchanans had a big backyard. There was plenty of work for shirtless Teo to do back there.

Eventually he went inside, and Jane had to find some other way to pass the time. She decided to brainstorm more ideas for her *Doctor Who/Veronica Mars* crossover fic. It was better than infinitely obsessing over Teo's attempt to kiss her last night.

If only there had been a couple of witnesses around, just to confirm that it really happened. Even if the kiss hadn't happened, Teo had definitely *tried* to make it happen. She had no clue how to interpret that. It was a good thing, but it left her feeling unsettled.

Margo came into the family room while Jane was trying to figure out the inner workings of Drunk Teo's brain. Their parents were out for the day, gone antiquing. Both of the girls were happy to have gotten out of it, even if their parents had tried to bribe them with lunch.

"What are you doing?" Margo asked.

"Brainstorming fan fiction."

Margo laughed. "Sounds like fun. I used to read a ton of *Battlestar Galactica* fic. Did I ever tell you that?"

"Oh my God," Jane said. "I've never watched that show, but I can't believe you read fan fiction!"

"I am a woman of many secrets."

"So many," Jane said, shaking her head.

Margo smiled. "You have to solemnly swear that you'll give *Battlestar Galactica* a try. It's such an awesome show."

"Only if you promise to send me a link to your favorite fic."

Margo held up her pinkie, and Jane hooked hers onto it.

"So you're really not going to tell Mom and Dad about last night?" Margo asked, settling back onto the couch and not looking Jane in the eye.

"I swear I won't. I'm not a monster. I'm not going to out you."

"I know. Or maybe I don't know. It all makes me really nervous."

Jane put her hands on Margo's shoulders. "I promise it's going to be okay."

"All right. But how do you know?"

Jane shrugged, then pulled the Magic 8 Ball from between the couch cushions. "Perhaps I could interest you in a conversation with the Magic 8?"

"Why did you have it down here with you?" Margo asked.

"I use it to make plot decisions."

"What will Mom and Dad say when they find out I'm bisexual?" Margo asked the ball.

"It doesn't work like that, dumb ass. You have to ask only yes-or-no questions."

"Oh, duh. I forgot." Margo thought for a second. "Will I be disowned when I come out?"

Very doubtful, the ball said.

"See," Jane said. "That's good news."

"I really don't think the Magic 8 knows our parents, but it does actually make me feel a little bit better."

"It always makes me feel a little bit better."

"Oh! Wait right here, one second," Margo said, running up the stairs.

"I don't know where else I would go," Jane called after her. She listened to the *thump-thump-thump* of Margo's feet in the second-floor hallway, and then the return trip.

Margo came back down the stairs and thrust a file folder into Jane's hands.

"Mom wanted me to give you these."

"College brochures? I didn't even know they still made physical college brochures."

"Some do, some don't. Mom has had most of these around the house for years. She thought maybe looking at them would help you feel less overwhelmed."

Jane looked over at Margo. "She's kind of grasping at straws."

"She says you're a visual learner."

"Why didn't she give them to me herself?"

"I'm assuming because she thought you would take them from me without too much complaint?"

Jane hummed and tossed the file aside.

"What is it with you and college, anyway?"

"Are you asking as an agent of Mom or because you're really interested?"

"Even if I was acting as an agent of Mom, I wouldn't tell her the answer. Especially not now, with the possibility of mutually assured destruction."

Jane's stomach twinged at that remark. "You really think I would blackmail you or something?"

"I don't know, Jane, I don't know anything anymore. I'm scared, okay."

Jane nodded. "Well, I promise I won't. And I'll answer your question, but you have to answer one of mine."

"Shoot."

"Does anyone else know you're bi?"

"Well, Kara Maxwell," Margo said, grinning.

"Besides Kara Maxwell."

"Some of my friends at school, my roommate. But not too many people. I haven't told any of my friends from high school because I wanted to come out to Mom and Dad first. I had this terrible image of them learning about this through some old-biddy gossiper, and I just—" Margo paused and shuddered. "I couldn't do that to them."

"They're going to be fine."

"Do you mind maybe being there when I come out?"

"Seriously? Of course I'll be there. I'll support you. I don't know how much help I'll actually be. But, yeah, of course."

Margo smiled.

"And now," Jane said, tapping on her laptop with a pencil to mimic a drumroll, "the real reason I'm terrified of college is that I think I'll fail."

"I don't think I realized you were terrified of college. I don't think Mom realizes that, either. I think she thinks you think—"

"Oh God, how we Connellys like to complicate things," Jane muttered.

"She thinks you're lazy. At least that's what I got out of it."

"I'm not lazy." Jane frowned. "Well, I am lazy, but it's not laziness that's keeping me from wanting to go to college. Maybe a little, but not about the work—about the getting there. The applications and the SATs. It's all really scary. It all seems like so much effort when I don't even know if it'll work out."

Margo nodded.

"And I have no clue what I'm going to do with my life, and I don't want Mom and Dad to waste their money so I can get straight Cs while getting a degree in English or what-ever."

"I mean, they don't have to waste their money. You could go where Mom works on the cheap and live at home."

Jane gave her sister a withering look.

"Right. That sounds awful. But you would still have to live at home even if you didn't go to college."

"I could find a full-time job and get an apartment."

"Yeah, right," Margo said, laughing. "Do you realize how much money you're talking about there? Rent, utilities, groceries. If you left home, there's no way Mom and Dad would still pay your cell-phone bill or your car insurance. You'd have so much money going out every month in bills you'd have to work three minimum-wage jobs just to stay afloat. It's not really that easy, Jane."

Jane deflated. "I know. But is it so bad that somehow that sounds easier than college? Like, what if I can't handle the workload?"

"You definitely won't be able to handle the workload of three jobs, either," Margo said.

"Everything is the worst."

"No, it's not. There's a plan in there somewhere. I'm sure of it. Maybe you could go to college close to home, but at a school where Mom doesn't work."

"What am I even going to take classes in?"

"Everything? Lots of people go to college undecided. Start out with a broad list. There must be something you like. Something you wouldn't mind pursuing."

Jane nodded. "You make it sound easier than it is in my head."

"Well, that's something."

"But it still fills me with this . . ." Jane paused, grasping for the right word. "Dread."

Margo sighed. "I'm sorry about that."

"I just want to find another way to do this, something that sounds doable to me. Something that doesn't make me wake up in the middle of the night in a cold sweat."

"Well, you could get a roommate," she said.

"I could," Jane said.

"You could get as many roommates as you needed so you wouldn't have to work three jobs. You'll find a way if this is what you really want."

Jane was on the verge of tears. "Thanks, Margo."

"I didn't mean to discourage you. I guess I don't understand. What you're talking about terrifies me. It terrifies most people our age. But you're braver than the rest of us. I wanted to make sure you weren't discarding the idea outright just because of the way Mom has presented it."

Jane knew that was a huge compliment, coming from her sister.

"All right. I'll think about it. But don't go telling Mom I said I'd think about it."

"She really does want what's best for you, even if she's not great at showing it."

"Maybe if she backed off a little, I'd be able to have some thoughts of my own."

Margo leaned over and gave her sister a longer-than-usual hug.

It wasn't until much later that night that Jane decided to at least look through the brochures. She felt better after talking to Margo, less panicked about the idea of going to college, but she still wasn't sure if it was really for her.

She flipped from one booklet to another, looking closely at a brochure for a small college in Virginia. She scanned the happy faces in a classroom full of students and smiled back at them. She read the caption beneath the photo: *Professor Mateo Rodriguez leads a first-year writing course.*

Jane bolted upright and stared at the face of the professor. The longer she stared, the more he looked like Teo.

Her Teo.

Could Connie have changed the father's name on Teo's birth certificate and then given her son the father's real name?

Jane's eyes crossed trying to figure that one out.

She leaped over to her laptop and started searching for *Mateo Rodriguez*, trying to find a link between him and Consuelo Garcia.

She'd heard of a couple of creepy sites that would show you

where people lived, but she'd been hesitant to try any of them out before this. Now that she had a concrete name and a picture that bore a striking resemblance to Teo, though, she couldn't stop herself.

She typed in the name *Mateo Rodriguez* and selected Virginia as his location. There were a few hits. She looked at each one for a long time. If she wanted pictures or exact addresses, she'd have to pay, but she was learning enough with the free information.

After some further searching, she found a Mateo Rodriguez who'd gone to high school with Connie.

But when she went to the website for the small college in Virginia, she couldn't find him on any of the faculty lists.

Jane cast a wider net, searching for Mateo Rodriguez in English departments across the country. But it was getting late and she wasn't having any luck.

After some thought, she made a new e-mail address—something less fandom-related than allonsygeronimor123@gmail.com—and composed an e-mail message to the English department, asking if she could find out where her favorite professor was now located, if that was okay. She would really appreciate a reference from him for grad school.

Lying isn't wrong if you're doing it to help someone else, she told herself.

She was about to turn off her light and go to sleep when she heard the water in the bathroom running and then the sound of bare feet padding past her bedroom. Margo was still awake.

Jane heaved herself out of bed and down the hall, knocking lightly on Margo's door.

"Come in."

"Hey," Jane said, leaning against the doorjamb.

Margo sat on her bed with her laptop open in front of her. She patted the spot next to her.

"What's up? Bad dream where Mom was chasing you with college applications while breathing fire?"

Jane laughed. "No, nothing like that. I need some advice. But it would mean that I have to tell you a big secret."

"Another big secret? Bigger than being afraid of college?"

"Yeah, and this one isn't my secret."

"Whose secret is it?"

"Teo's."

"You sure you want to betray his trust?"

"Well, that's the thing. He doesn't know that I know, and I could really use someone to talk to about it."

"All right. What is it?"

"Teo's been looking for his dad, and he doesn't know that I know, but I might have found him."

"Seriously?" Margo asked.

Jane filled her sister in on the research she'd been doing, showed her the college brochure with the picture of Mateo Rodriguez and told her about the e-mail she'd just sent.

"Jane, this is a really big deal."

"I know."

"Do you think it's a good idea to keep looking?"

"I'm so close."

"I don't know, Janie. It doesn't feel like any of your business." Margo wasn't sure she could come up with any other way to say it, but she really wasn't sure Jane should get involved.

Jane sighed. "I know, but I want to help. He's been so great this summer and . . ." She paused, unsure of how to explain the next part. "He tried to kiss me the other night at the party."

"No way! Why didn't you tell me?"

"Because there were bigger things going on. And it was sort of embarrassing for him, because he missed. Like, he leaned over and fell off his chair."

Margo shuddered. "I just got a serious case of secondhand embarrassment."

Jane nodded and scrunched up her nose. "But something is happening between us. And I want to give this to him. This news."

Margo was torn. "Fine, but just be careful."

"I will be," Jane said, standing up and walking to the door. "Thanks for not telling me not to do it, though."

Margo nodded and smiled and hoped this wouldn't come back to bite her sister in the ass.

Chapter 14

JANE'S SMILE WAS THE FIRST THING TEO NOTICED WHEN HE got home from work on Monday afternoon. He was relieved that she wasn't annoyed with him and that even though he'd barely left her side on Saturday night, she would still smile when she saw him.

He hadn't worn out his welcome.

Or completely and entirely humiliated himself with the missed kiss.

"Hiya," she said. She was cleaning up crumbs on the kitchen table, and the sun was streaming through the window in such a way that it threw her profile into sharp relief. Teo had this weird feeling like they were playing house, but he shook it off.

"Hey," he said, picking his way through the crumbs on the floor to stand next to her.

"Welcome to the madhouse."

"You have a . . ." He paused to pick a Cheerio from her hair.

"Yeah, it's been one of those days. I had this brilliant idea to let the girls make their own edible necklaces, and it kind of ended with a whole lot of mess."

"I'll help." Teo turned around and got the broom and dustpan out of the closet.

"Thanks," she said. "I owe you one."

"Nah."

"Yeah," she said in the same tone as his.

"You were really nice to Drunk Teo on Saturday night. You could have left him, abandoned on the edge of the beach, to fend for himself. But you didn't. And therefore, since you helped me clean up my mess, I'll help you clean up yours."

"You really weren't a mess on Saturday," Jane said, shrugging. "You were actually kind of, um . . ."

Teo looked over at her from where he was sweeping.

"You were kind of adorable," she said, hiding her eyes behind her hand.

"Really?"

"Really."

"Huh," Teo said, concentrating on his sweeping for a minute, staring at the floor. "So I have to ask."

"Yeah?" Jane said.

"Where exactly are my sisters? What did you do with them? I feel like they should be here helping you clean."

"Oh. Them. They were helping me, but that's how the floor

got so messy, so I released them from their duties and they're in the basement."

"Makes sense."

"They really were making the whole process harder."

Teo leaned on the broom handle. "I can totally imagine that."

Jane opened her mouth and then closed it, turning back to intently scraping smashed Twizzlers off the table.

For the rest of the week following the party, Jane always seemed to have something on the tip of her tongue—something she wanted to say but couldn't for whatever reason.

Teo almost asked her about it several times. But how do you even ask a question like that? He couldn't begin to get the phrasing right, never mind actually say the words "Is there something you want to tell me?"

On Saturday afternoon when Jane texted to see if Teo was around and if he wanted to take a walk, he felt a crackle in the air, like something was about to change. He was ready.

He waited for Jane on his front steps, and she came around the corner a minute later.

"Hey," Teo said. "It's nice to see you off duty."

Jane laughed. "It's nice to see you off duty, too."

"We do seem to spend a lot of time at each other's places of employment."

They walked for a few minutes without saying much. Their hands brushed a few times, and Teo thought about twining his fingers with hers more than once, but he wanted to hear what Jane had to say before he did anything like that.

"So is this a social visit or something else?" he asked.

"Ah, well, I guess it depends on how you look at it," Jane said. "I was kind of waiting for today, when I knew we could hang out without the girls around, to talk to you."

She pulled a folded-up piece of glossy paper out of her back pocket and handed it to Teo.

"What is this? Is this a college brochure?" Teo asked, holding it like it was some kind of rare, ancient artifact.

"Yes."

"Why would you bring a college brochure on our walk?" he asked.

"Well . . ."

"Is this where you're going to school?" Teo asked. He mentally prepared to be excited for Jane, even though the college was in northern Virginia, nowhere near any school Teo was planning to apply to. He would miss her.

"No, it's not where I'm going to school. The jury's still out on that," Jane said.

"About where to go or . . . ?" Teo trailed off.

"About if I even want to go," Jane muttered.

They had walked to the elementary school playground without really meaning to, so they took a seat on the merry-go-round.

"Why wouldn't you go to college?" Teo asked, genuinely flummoxed by the idea. He'd been dreaming about escaping to college his entire life.

"I don't know. It's a long story."

"I've got time," Teo said, leaning against one of the bars.

"But that's not what we're here to talk about," Jane said, perking up. "And I didn't bring this brochure to show you the school. I wanted to show you this picture." Jane's hands were visibly shaking when she took the pamphlet from Teo and opened it up, pointing at a small picture in one corner.

Teo read the caption beneath the picture three times before the significance of it sank in.

"I think I found your dad," Jane said.

"Why would you think he's my dad?" Teo asked, staring at the picture. Even without closely examining it he saw the resemblance, but he didn't want to admit that to Jane. The smile on the man's face was like a punch in the gut.

"I don't know."

Teo shook his head and huffed out a breath.

"Wait, I do know," Jane continued. "Because he went to high school with your mom and he used to live in New Jersey. He has the same last name as the dad listed on your birth certificate."

"How do you know anything about my birth certificate?"

Jane stood up, crossing her arms.

"Let me start over. I saw a search on your computer one day when the girls were playing hide-and-seek. I thought they were in your room. A couple of windows were open on your computer. I didn't even mean to look at it, your search for how to find your biological parent, but it was hard to miss. I couldn't stop thinking about it. I wasn't snooping, I swear."

"What?" Teo asked, narrowing his eyes.

"You've been so nice this summer; I wanted to help you with this. I thought I could find him. Once I saw him in this brochure, I had to do a little digging, but I finally found him in Illinois."

"I don't understand how this is any of your business."

"I thought you wanted to find him. And you mentioned that you feel left out," Jane spluttered.

"I can't believe you did this. That you brought this to me." He was yelling, and Jane cringed away from him. Teo crumpled up the paper and threw it in the dirt.

He stood and loomed over her, and Jane backed up a step. He stared at her, but she didn't stare back. She looked like he had slapped her. This wasn't his fault, and it wasn't fair of her to look so abused.

"I didn't really do anything," she said. "I looked at your birth certificate. I asked my mom a couple of questions, but she didn't know anything about your dad. Or at least she pretended not to know anything. Then this guy basically fell into my lap. I did some more searching. I knew where to look—"

"Oh, yeah, you didn't do anything," Teo said, interrupting. "You didn't go through our stuff; you didn't snoop on my computer. You didn't talk to your mom?" Teo's temples were pulsing. The more he thought about all the ways Jane had broken his trust, the angrier he felt.

"I did do all that. But I wanted to help you. You're always helping me. I thought I could do something for you. To thank you."

Teo rubbed his hands over his face. "How dare you?" he bit out.

"I'm sorry. I thought you'd be happy. I wouldn't have done it if I had thought you wouldn't be happy."

"You wouldn't have done it if you had thought at all," Teo spat out. "But thinking isn't always your strong suit."

Her chin quivered. He had crossed a line and he couldn't go back. Maybe he didn't want to go back.

"Shit, Jane," Teo said.

"No, shut up. Just shut up. I said I was sorry. You don't have to do anything about it. It's not like I contacted him on your behalf."

"Thank God for small favors," Teo said.

Jane gave him a dirty look. "I thought that's what you wanted. I thought you would be happy." A tear rolled down her cheek, and Teo felt himself choking up at the sight of it.

"You have no clue what I want."

"But—"

He couldn't do this. He couldn't listen to her for one more second. So he ran.

He ran as far and as fast as he could. He kept running until he barely recognized where he was, until he'd lost all track of time.

And then he ran home.

On his way there, he considered asking his mom about his dad. Maybe it was time for answers. Real answers. Not some theory Jane Connelly had cooked up.

But it wasn't something he and his mom had ever talked about.

He stopped running to catch his breath. He was only a few blocks from home now, and he needed to calm down. But every time he tried to collect his thoughts, they would spiral out of control again.

Because when he was a kid, Teo *had* asked about his dad, and his mom had always told him that they were fine alone, that they didn't need anyone else. Teo had believed her for a long time. At least until Buck came into the picture and it became apparent that they hadn't been fine, just the two of them.

Until Buck came into the picture and renovated their house.

Until Buck came into the picture and they stopped speaking Spanish.

Until Buck came into the picture and suddenly there were little girls all over the house, with their princess dresses and My Little Ponies.

He took that last one back because he really did love his sisters. It was Buck he had a problem with. Buck and his mom—they were the ones to blame for how he was feeling. And Jane, for bringing this to his attention and making it an issue. Jane had no clue what she was doing, but that didn't make her innocent.

Teo punched a stop sign because it seemed like a better idea than going home and punching Buck. But punching a stop sign was a terrible idea, and it hurt like hell.

He stumbled home, thankful when he got there that no one was around. There was a note on the table—the whole family was at the pool, if he wanted to join them.

He went up to his room and threw himself face-first onto his bed. He had never been so pissed off in his entire life, and he had no clue what to do about it.

Chapter 15

Jane spent the rest of the weekend debating whether or not to quit her job.

She tried to drown her sorrows in fan fiction, but not even the latest *Doctor Who/Anne of Green Gables* crossover could soothe her.

The scene with Teo had been that bad. She couldn't imagine ever having to see him again, never mind having to talk to him, to be civil.

He had every right to say what he'd said—it really wasn't any of her business—but that didn't mean Jane needed to go back for more. If Jane had taken a few more days to think about telling him, if she hadn't become so excited when an e-mail came back from the college in Virginia telling her that Mateo Rodriguez now worked in Illinois, maybe things would be different.

If only Jane had listened to Margo and taken her warnings more seriously.

But all Jane could see was Teo's smiling face when she told him she had found his father. She kept imagining the moment in her head, and it went nothing like what had happened at the playground.

As soon as she'd seen the dawning realization on his face as he read the caption, she knew she'd made the wrong decision. But at that point there was no way to stop it. By the time she knew she'd made a mistake, Teo already understood what was going on.

Over the past month, Teo had become one of her favorite people. Without Ravi around, he was awesome. He was fun and reliable, always willing to hang out. It was obvious to Jane that part of it was Teo's nature: He hated being alone. So, sure, maybe he was using her, but Jane didn't mind. She didn't exactly have friends beating down her door, either. There were worse people to spend time with than Teo Garcia. Losing him as a friend was the worst part of this misunderstanding. Even worse than losing whatever might have been *happening* between them.

There had to be some way to fix this.

On Sunday night, Jane spent hours with her trusty Magic 8 Ball. She had a long list of yes-or-no questions about this shitstorm with Teo, and she asked every single one of them, even if they were sort of redundant.

"Does Teo hate me?"

It is decidedly so.

"Will he hate me forever?"

Better not tell you now.

"Will Teo ever forgive me?"

Outlook good.

"Should I text him and apologize?"

Reply hazy, try again.

Jane refocused on the question.

"Should I text him and apologize?"

Reply hazy, try again.

Jane groaned in frustration. She really wanted an answer to this question. Apologizing was something she could do right away. Maybe it would make her feel better to contact him on her own terms.

The fourth time the ball told her *Reply hazy, try again*, she decided to move on to a different line of questioning.

"Did I make a huge mistake?"

Without a doubt.

"Can I make it up to him?"

Yes, definitely.

"I wish you could tell me how to make it up to him," she said to the Magic 8. It was great for answering questions but terrible at giving advice.

Monday arrived faster than it usually did, as if Jane had blinked and it had gone from Sunday afternoon directly to Monday morning.

When Jane arrived at the Buchanans', Teo had already left for work. She knew she would probably see him in the afternoon, so she prepared herself all day, but then he never came home.

The guilt she felt about their fight hung over her head like a rain cloud. The first few days that week, Teo was out of the house when she arrived and didn't come home until after she had left.

On Thursday, Connie got stuck in traffic, and Jane was still at the house when Teo came through the back door.

He froze.

"Hey, wow," Jane said. "I didn't think I'd get to see you."

He stared at her.

"I'm happy to see you. I know neither of us is much for confrontation, but we should talk."

He crossed his arms.

"I just want to say how sorry I am," Jane continued.

He raised his eyebrows, and they stood there looking at each other as the seconds dragged by. Jane's discomfort grew unbearable, and she had to look away.

"I don't really know what else to say if you don't say anything back," she mumbled at the floor. "I really am sorry. I don't know how to make you believe me."

When she looked up, he was gone, walking quickly into the living room and up the stairs, where he knew Jane wouldn't follow, no matter how much she wanted to.

By Saturday afternoon, Jane couldn't keep her feelings in for one second longer. While she was out with Margo, running errands for their mom, she finally blurted out, "I had a big fight with Teo and we're not speaking and I don't know if we're ever going to speak again." They were at the grocery store; they'd already stopped at the dry cleaner's and the library.

"What did you fight about?" Margo asked.

"The dad thing. Of course you were right."

"I promise I didn't want to be right," Margo said.

"I know. I really thought Teo would be so psyched," Jane said. "But when I told him, he blew up at me. And I tried to apologize again the other day, figuring he needed time to cool off, but he walked out of the room. Didn't even say a word."

"That sucks," Margo said.

"Are you any closer to telling Mom and Dad your news?"

"Quite the subject change," Margo noted.

"I don't really want to start crying about Teo in the frozen-food aisle."

Margo patted her shoulder sympathetically and followed Jane's lead. "Not really. If anything, I've kind of stopped thinking about it. It's not that big a deal, right? And maybe I'll fall for a guy and they'll never have to know."

Jane made a face. "Is that really what you want?"

"No. Not even a little. But I don't want them to—" Margo stopped short and shook her head. "I don't know. I don't want them to be mad at me."

Jane had no clue how to respond to that. As much as she wanted to tell Margo that everything would be okay, she knew it would be like shouting into the abyss. Margo had dug in her heels and really believed that their parents would disown her. More than that, though, Jane had a feeling that Margo was worried their parents wouldn't *like* her anymore.

"So what's next on the list?" Jane asked.

"Aluminum cake pans," Margo read off the shopping list their mom had written.

They wandered up and down aisles they had already been through a dozen times until finally they located the aluminum bakeware at the back of the store. When Margo gasped, Jane stopped scanning the wall of throwaway pans to look at her.

At the end of the pet food aisle stood Kara Maxwell.

Margo's eyes went wide.

"When was the last time you talked to her?" Jane asked as they moved out of Kara's line of sight.

"Not since the party. But it feels like an omen that she just happens to be at the grocery store at the same time we're here."

"I kind of agree." Jane peeked up the aisle again, and Kara was still there.

"Only 'kind of'?" Margo asked. "If I asked the Magic 8, it would totally agree."

Jane pretended to shake a Magic 8 Ball and check the answer. "'Outlook good.'"

"Should I go talk to her?"

"'Without a doubt,'" Jane said, making her eyes as wide as Margo's.

"What are you going to do?"

"Wander around the grocery store and pretend I don't know you while actually watching your interaction from every possible angle."

Margo shrugged. "That sounds completely normal, and I'll want a full report in the car."

Jane did exactly as she'd promised, going full-on Veronica Mars, catching bits and pieces of Margo and Kara's conversation as she made several circuits of the store. In a funny architectural phenomenon, if she stood by the packaged deli meats, she could hear almost every word they said, but she couldn't actually see them and they couldn't see her. She did a few drive-bys with the cart so she could also report to Margo on their body language.

"I actually have to go back to school soon," Kara was saying at one point.

"Bummer," Margo said.

"Yeah, field hockey practice starts next week."

"Oh, wow," Margo said. Jane had a feeling that Margo didn't even know what field hockey was.

"Sucks that we don't go to school in the same state."

"Sucks that we don't go to school in the same time zone."

The next time Jane came around, they were obviously wrapping up their conversation.

". . . winter break," Kara was saying as Jane moved into hearing distance.

"Yeah," Margo said, squeezing Kara's arm. "That would be great."

Kara leaned in to hug her, and then they said good-bye.

While they checked out, Margo was practically bouncing. "Isn't it kind of amazing when you like someone for a really long time and then they suddenly like you back?"

"I can't say I've actually experienced that, but it sounds incredible."

"Well, when you do, come talk to me, and we can revel in the freaking awesomeness of it together."

"That good, huh?" Jane asked as she manipulated the cart out to the car.

"Definitely," Margo said. She babbled about Kara the whole time while they were loading bags into the trunk.

"So are you and Kara going to have a long-distance relationship or something?" Jane asked, taking the driver's seat. She flat-out refused to let Margo drive anymore.

"No, but we'll see each other during winter break. I don't think we're destined to be together forever, but it's good. It gives me a little more confidence in everything."

"That's great."

"It feels like an omen. And I think I should definitely come out to Mom and Dad tonight. I needed to be reminded of how much better it will feel when I'm honest with them."

"I like that idea a lot more than never telling them and hoping you find a decent guy," Jane said.

"Yeah, that idea was terrible," Margo agreed.

"It would have been super awkward for everyone involved."

"I know it could still happen. But until now, I was sort of hypothetically bi. I mean, quite frankly, I'm only hypothetically sexual, even. I don't exactly have a ton of experience," Margo said, looking at her hands.

"Me neither," Jane said.

"Yeah, but you're still in high school. It's downright pathetic to be almost twenty-one and barely ever kissed."

"Everyone's different," Jane said.

"Thanks for that one, Jane. I would never have come up with that on my own."

"Sorry, I guess it's one of those clichéd things people say because it's true."

Margo nodded and then continued her very excited monologue about Kara and her sexuality and living life to the fullest.

They were nearly home when she finally noticed how quiet Jane was.

"I'm sorry about Teo," Margo said.

"Thanks."

"I'm sure you guys will work it out."

"Do you have any advice?" Jane asked. "This time I promise to listen."

"Oh, now you *want* my advice," Margo teased.

Jane smiled grimly as she pulled the car into the driveway.

"Give him time, Janie. It's a lot to take in under the best of circumstances. He'll come around. He likes you too much not to."

Jane nodded, took a deep breath, and helped her sister take the groceries into the house. There wasn't much else for her to do.

Chapter 16

A WEEK HAD PASSED SINCE HIS BLOWUP WITH JANE, AND TEO finally had to acknowledge that he missed her. He didn't know what to do about missing her, but at least he could admit to himself that he did. That was a big step, considering that forty-eight hours earlier, he'd still sort of hated her.

"I messed up," he told Ravi on the phone that afternoon. He had no clue whether Ravi was listening, but he needed to say it.

"How?" Ravi asked.

"It's a really long story, and I need you to listen and not judge."

"If you had any kind of sex with Jane Connelly, I don't want to hear about it."

"I did not have any kind of sex with Jane Connelly. Why would you even go there?"

"I saw the pictures from that party, Teo. You were all up in each other's business that night."

"Well, it does have to do with Jane, but nothing about sex."

Ravi sighed. "Fine. Tell me."

Teo filled him in on every last detail of his argument with Jane last weekend. When Teo finally finished, Ravi whistled long and low. "Dude, that's a lot to take in."

"I know," Teo said.

"And, oh God, I hate saying this, but I have to."

"What?"

"You know, this is legit painful for me to even form these words."

"Say it."

"She was trying to help you. It sucks how she went about it, but I'm pretty sure her intentions were sound." And then he paused for a beat. "Even if she is an idiot."

"Oh God, I suck so bad." Teo covered his eyes with his hand.

"You don't really suck that bad. But, like, what do you want to do?"

"About the dad thing?"

"Obviously."

"I have no freaking clue."

"Do you want to meet him?"

"I want to stop hating him."

"Are you going to make up with Jane?"

"I have to. I kind of miss her."

Ravi made dramatic retching noises.

"And I freaked out on her because I'm mad at him. I want to make sure she knows that. But I do think I need to find him. To actually see him. To stop hating the idea of him or whatever."

"Well, I can't exactly help you in any way, shape, or form, since I'm approximately eight billion miles away, but let me know if I can do anything."

"Thanks, man."

"You know it."

They wrapped up their phone call. Ravi might not be able to help, but Teo knew who could.

Which is how he ended up ringing Jane Connelly's doorbell on Saturday night.

Jane didn't hear the conversation happening at the front door, nor did she hear the footsteps on the stairs, or the person approaching her bedroom.

She barely even heard the first knock—that was how into writing she was.

At the second knock, she minimized the window and clicked on the nail art how-to videos she always kept open in a separate browser so that when her mom looked over her shoulder, she would never catch Jane reading something she would deem inappropriate. Or, worse, writing something she would deem inappropriate.

"Come in!" Jane called when her screen was clear.

"It's locked," a familiar voice said. A familiar *male* voice.

"Teo?" Jane got up and went to open the door.

"Hi," he said. "Your mom told me I could come up."

"That's weird," Jane said.

"Well, she also told me to tell you to keep your door open while I'm 'visiting.'" Teo put air quotes around the last word.

"She makes it sound like you're here for a conjugal." Jane put her hand over her mouth.

Teo's jaw dropped for a second, and then he broke into a grin.

"That was just—I don't know—I am—so . . ." Jane shook her head and couldn't seem to finish a sentence. "My mother would not be pleased with that kind of talk."

Teo nodded and then looked a little shy. "So, hey."

"Oh, hey, hi, what's up, how are you?" Jane seriously considered slapping herself in the face for her extreme awkwardness.

Teo smiled. "You okay?"

"Oh, just great. Yeah. Totally awesome. Spent most of the past week feeling like I'd swallowed a grapefruit while you studiously ignored me."

"I wasn't ignoring you."

"You wouldn't even look at me."

"Well, I'm here now. Looking at you. Ready to apologize for blowing you off."

"I accept," she said. "Even though I need to apologize more."

Jane sat down in her computer chair, and Teo looked around, hoping to find somewhere to sit besides Jane's bed. Jane finally took pity on him and dragged Margo's desk chair in from her room down the hall.

"Thanks," Teo said.

"I couldn't stop thinking about all the ways I could have done this differently, or better. I want you to know I've learned my lesson. I will not meddle in your life, or anyone else's, ever again."

"Listen," Teo said. "It's okay. Or if it's not exactly okay, it's forgivable. I forgive you. I don't want to fight with you. I'm more mad at him than I am at you, for the record."

She smiled, obviously relieved. "I don't want to fight with you, either. And I really did think I was helping you."

Teo nodded.

"I wanted to ask you about the search when I saw it on my first day of work. But we weren't really friends. And then in my head it seemed like an awesome idea to find him for you. I knew I could." Jane paused. "And now I'll stop defending myself, since you already forgave me."

"Good plan," Teo said. "I'm sorry I ran away from you like that."

Jane looked at the slump in his shoulders, and guilt rose in her chest, making her throat constrict. She tried to clear it, but her "No big deal" came out choked.

"And I'm sorry I said that thing about, um . . ." He paused and shook his head before turning to look at Jane. She felt his eyes on her but kept her gaze focused on the fake wood grain of her desk. "That thing about thinking not being your strong suit. That was way out of line."

Jane laughed and scrunched up her nose. "Was it out of line? I thought you hit the nail on the head."

"No way. You're really good at thinking. You're super logical."

"Not really, but thanks for that."

"Seriously, Jane," Teo said. "I mean, you tracked this guy down and figured out he was related to me without even trying—it's impressive. I've been trying to find him for years and never even got close."

"Well, you said yourself that you were only casually looking."

"But you made it seem so easy. I'm not saying I tried hard, but you barely tried at all and found the answers."

"It was the pamphlet. I didn't do much except not want to go to college, so my mom gave me college propaganda."

Teo smiled. "You just can't take the compliment, huh? No matter how hard I shove one at you, you keep shoving it away."

Jane stared at him. "You're complimenting me?"

"Yes, Jane. That's what complimenting is. Recognizing things that people are good at and telling them you're impressed."

"Huh. I guess I never really thought of it like that." Jane smiled. "Thanks for not hating me even though I totally stuck my nose where it didn't belong."

"Thanks for not hating me even though I reacted like a complete dick."

"See, that's the thing. You reacted like a dick, but that doesn't mean you *are* a dick. It's a very important distinction."

Teo smiled, too, and took a deep breath. "There's something I kind of wanted to ask you about."

"Sure," Jane said, feeling more confident than she had in a long time.

"Do you have any advice? About the dad search?"

"Seriously? Haven't I done enough damage?"

"I don't think you really did any damage. I think you kind of brought this idea of finding my dad, actually finding him and meeting him, into reality. I liked to look for him when Buck was on my case about something, or when I felt left out of family crap. But now my father doesn't have to be a fantasy."

"Oh. Okay." Jane leaned her chin in her hand. "Does your mom know you're looking?"

Teo shook his head.

"Oh, wow." Jane took a deep breath. "Does anyone?"

"I filled Ravi in, but that's it." He gave her his very best puppy-dog look. "Will you help me?"

She couldn't say no. "What do you want to find out, specifically?"

"Where is he? Where is Mateo Rodriguez?"

"He works in Illinois now. At the University of Illinois Urbana-Champaign campus."

"How did you manage to work out that he wasn't in Virginia?"

"Well, I went on the university website and tried to find him. When I couldn't, I e-mailed the English department and asked if they knew where Mateo Rodriguez was teaching now. I said I was a former student and wanted to get a recommendation from him."

"And that worked?"

"Yes. I got an e-mail back a few days later."

"And you still don't think you're smart enough to go to college?"

Jane lifted her chin. "I never said I wasn't smart enough, just that I thought I might fail. You can be smart and still fail."

"Very true," Teo said.

"Anyway, I didn't get much further than that. I haven't even checked the website for the University of Illinois. I could still be wrong."

"But you're probably not wrong."

"He might not be your father."

"Yeah, I know. It says Jose Rodriguez on my birth certificate."

"I know. I've thought about that. It's such a common name. I kind of wonder if your mom changed it. Or if maybe his name is Jose Mateo Rodriguez and he goes by his middle name."

"I hadn't considered that."

Jane was about to say something else when Teo continued.

"What if he doesn't want to meet me?" Teo asked.

"Whoa there," Jane said, holding up her hands. "I feel like we skipped about a thousand steps. There are a lot of other things to do before you even consider meeting him."

"Like what kind of steps?"

"Like confirming where he is. Contacting him. Deciding if *you* want to meet *him*."

"Do you think I want to meet him?"

"I definitely can't answer that question for you. But, like, three minutes ago you told me you were mad at him."

"Just because I'm mad at him doesn't mean I don't want to meet him." He gestured toward her computer. "Can we look him up? Together?"

"Yeah, sure," Jane said. She brought up the window she'd been working in earlier; completely forgetting that her fan fiction document was open.

Teo squinted at the screen. "'Doctor, you know we can't go back in time and save Lilly,'" Teo read. "What is that?"

"Um, nothing," Jane said, closing tabs and blushing furiously.

"Were you writing a story? I didn't know you did anything creative."

"Um . . . well, yes."

"What was it? What kind of doctor? Now I'm curious."

"We should concentrate on your thing. I'm sure you have plans tonight. Going out, picking up some hotties."

"I have nothing to do," Teo said, leaning back in the chair and lacing his hands behind his head casually. "I want to hear about your creative streak."

"Gah. Fine. I write *Doctor Who* crossover fan fiction."

"I don't know what any of that means."

"Do you know what *Doctor Who* is?"

"Some British TV show?"

"It is way more than that, but yes. It's a TV show. Do you know what fan fiction is?"

"Yes."

"Okay. So I write *Doctor Who* fan fiction mixed with bits and pieces of other TV shows or books or movies."

"So what's that one a crossover with?"

"*Veronica Mars.*"

"Never heard of it."

"Do you live under a rock?"

"I don't watch much TV."

"You need to watch TV! And you definitely need to watch both of these shows. It is a requirement for being my friend."

He held up his hands in surrender. "You're very serious about this."

"I am! We would put on an episode right now if we didn't have other things to concentrate on."

"I promise to watch at least one episode of both of those shows with you."

"Thank you," she said, shaking her head. "It's a shame what this world is coming to."

"Aren't there, like, a billion seasons of *Doctor Who*?"

"Not quite."

"I still don't get it."

"Then stop bothering me about it, and let's talk about your dad search."

"I guess. But I'm going to get to the bottom of this crossfit fanover thing."

"You sound like my grandmother."

"She's a lovely woman. How is she these days?"

"She died three years ago."

"Oh. Wow. I do remember that. Sorry for your loss."

Jane rolled her eyes. "Thank you. Now can we get down to business?"

"Yeah. Just tell me whether he's really in Illinois. I know you're right, that I have a lot of other things to deal with first. But if I know where this guy is, he might seem more real."

"You can't run off and find him—you know that, right? Like, no matter what we learn right now, you should think about it a little. And definitely contact him before you do anything."

"What would the Magic 8 Ball say?" Teo asked, picking it up off the shelf above Jane's desk.

"Give it a whirl," Jane said.

"Should I find my dad?" Teo asked.

"What does it say?" Jane asked.

Teo showed her the window, carefully turning it so the answer wouldn't change or disappear. *Ask again later.*

Jane shrugged. "We'll have to keep going without the wisdom of the Magic 8 for now."

By the time Teo left, he had learned that Mateo Rodriguez definitely worked at the University of Illinois and was teaching a literature class five days a week over the summer. And Teo was going to track him down.

Chapter 17

ON TEO'S DAY OFF, WHICH HAPPENED TO BE WEDNESDAY THAT week, Jane mentioned that she wanted to take the girls mini golfing before the summer ended.

"There's another month until school starts."

"Yeah, but I'm done babysitting in two weeks," she reminded Teo.

"All right. Let's take them mini golfing today," he said, standing up from the sofa.

"Right now?"

"Sure."

"You don't mind spending your day off like this?"

"Hell, no. I love those little weirdos."

"Awesome. I really appreciate your going with me. I foresee a long afternoon of fishing their balls out of water features."

"You've never seen my sisters golf. They're actually really good."

"I'll believe it when I see it."

Jane and Teo rounded up the girls and got them settled in the van.

"Are we going to the good golf course at the boardwalk?" Keegan asked as she was buckling her seat belt.

"Yes," Jane said.

"Yay!" all three girls yelled.

Teo put his hands over his ears. "You guys are so loud."

He should have known better; acknowledging their loudness just made them yell louder.

Teo had not been kidding—Jane couldn't believe what good golfers the three girls were. They were leagues ahead of her, getting bored when it took Jane six strokes to sink the ball.

"I hate to admit how much better they are than I am," Jane said after she shooed them on to the next hole. "Why are they so good?"

"When my mom and Buck go on vacation, they always golf, so they made sure the girls love to golf, too."

"I'm totally slowing you guys down. You can go ahead, too," she said.

"Nah, I'm good."

"I feel like you're paying too much attention to me. I'm getting all nervous." She wiped her palms on her shorts.

"I'll distract you. Did you write any new fan stories lately?"

She rolled her eyes and smiled over at him. "You know, if this was fan fiction, you would try to show me how to adjust my hands on my club to make my swing more potent."

"You know, Jane," Teo said, "I could give you some pointers to make your swing more potent."

Jane laughed, figuring that Teo was teasing her, until he actually stepped toward her and her breath caught in her throat.

"Unless you don't want me to," Teo said, backing off when he sensed her tension.

"No, no. I could probably use some pointers."

Teo stood behind her, leaning in close, unnecessarily close. He felt like he was playing a part, but it was a part he liked, a part he wasn't used to playing. It wasn't anything he'd ever felt comfortable trying before, but it was different with Jane.

"So you put your hands like this," Teo said, manipulating her thumbs and fingers. "And loosen up a little. You're too stiff."

Jane tried to loosen up, but she seemed to have forgotten how movement worked and instead kind of wiggled her butt and kept her legs completely straight.

"Jane," Teo said, stepping to her side, figuring he might as well take the opportunity to teach her a better stance. "Like this." He bounced a little, loosening his joints and holding his hands the way she should.

"Okay, I think I get it," Jane said.

Teo wrapped his arms around her again, and she closed her eyes, allowing herself to relax against him. But as they were about to take the stroke, they heard a big splash up ahead.

"Hey, you two lovebirds!" A guy who worked at the mini golf course was calling to them. "I think one of your kids fell into the pond."

"Oh my God! Keegan!" Jane cried, tearing herself out of Teo's arms and running across the greens and through other people's shots. She paid no attention to the path—she just wanted to get to the poor little girl sitting in the too-blue water.

Teo ran a few steps behind Jane, kicking off his flip-flops, preparing to go in and rescue his sister. But when he and Jane reached Keegan, she was already standing up and walking toward the bank.

"What happened?" Jane asked.

"I was trying to see if the water felt as blue as it looked," Keegan explained. Teo lifted her out of the water, and she wrapped her legs around his waist. Teo hugged her close, not caring about the blue water staining his shirt.

"It's okay," he said.

"Oh, I know," Keegan said, leaning back. "And it didn't feel as blue as it looked."

Piper and Rory trotted over then, and the group got ready to leave.

"But we didn't finish playing!" Rory complained.

"Keegan needs to change," Jane said.

"Fine," Rory grumbled.

"Next time I want to go in the pond!" Piper said.

Teo shook his head.

Before he and Jane got into the car, he pulled on her arm

to stop her. "Do you want to hang out sometime without my sisters? Someplace besides your house or my house or the town pool?"

"Um, definitely," Jane said, biting her lip to keep from smiling too much.

"Maybe this weekend?"

Jane nodded. She wished she could speed things up and get to that point where she was allowed to kiss Teo. She had a feeling it was coming, but they weren't there yet.

Which didn't mean she could stop thinking about it.

By Saturday afternoon, Jane felt like she couldn't hold it in a second longer. She and Margo lounged on the sofa, watching TV.

"Teo asked me to go on a date tonight," Jane whispered to her sister. She hadn't even really meant to say it. It was as if the words overflowed from her mouth.

"Really?"

"Yeah, he asked me on Wednesday."

"No way!" Margo said. "I can't believe you held it in that long."

Jane smiled. "I didn't want to jinx it by talking about it too much. I think it's a date. I mean, maybe it isn't. But I think it might be."

"I figured you'd made up when he stopped by the house the other night, but I never got a chance to ask you about it."

"I think something's *happening*," Jane said.

"I can't believe you're the same person who, mere weeks ago, refused to even admit that she liked Teo."

Jane sank deeper into the cushions. "I really, really like him. I don't even know when it happened. But this week has been downright magical."

"How?" Margo asked.

"Oh, just with him asking me out. And he's around more. After last week I was starting to worry that we'd never talk again, and then he finally came around."

Their mother called them for dinner.

"Where's Dad?" Margo asked as she sat down.

"Working late," their mom said.

They were barely two bites into the meal when she started nagging Jane. "We really need to talk about college," she said.

"I know," Jane said. "I've been working on a plan."

"Really?" her mom asked.

Jane took a deep breath. "Yeah, I've been thinking about it, and even though I'm still not completely sure that college is for me, I know I need to at least apply to keep my options open. But I'd really like to get a job and maybe a couple of roommates after graduation. I don't know what I want to do with my life. It seems like a waste of time and money to go to college without a purpose." Jane sat up straight, proud of herself for having something prepared this time.

"And what would you do for health insurance?" her mother asked.

"I don't know. Can't I stay on yours? Or if I find a full-time job, won't I have insurance?"

Her mother rolled her eyes. "And what about utilities and paying for your car?"

"I'd have a job. Therefore, I would have money. And remember the part about roommates?"

"And who are these hypothetical roommates? Where would you find them?"

"I don't know. Craigslist?"

"You will not live with anyone you meet on Craigslist," her mother said, slamming her fist on the dining room table.

"Lots of people find roommates on Craigslist."

"Not my seventeen-year-old daughter."

"For starters, I'll be eighteen then, and you won't have as much say in the matter. But I know how to find a roommate responsibly."

"You will end up living in a crack den."

Jane shook her head. "You have no faith in me."

"I want what's best for you! Why is this so hard for you to understand?"

"I want what's best for me, too. I've come up with a plan that I'm comfortable with. And in six months, or two years, or ten years, maybe I'll decide I do want to go to college, but I need to make my own decisions about my life right now."

"This is unacceptable."

"You told me I needed a plan, and I laid one out to you. A completely reasonable plan."

"How is it reasonable?" her mother asked, shaking her head.

"I'll have money, food, a place to live."

"It isn't what I want for you."

"Why won't you listen to me? This is what *I* want for me," Jane said. "You never listen."

Without another glance, Jane pushed herself away from the table and ran upstairs. She hated herself for it. That wasn't how a mature adult would behave. But she hated her mother more.

She paced her room, tossing her Magic 8 from one hand to the other until there was a knock on her door and Margo peered in.

"That sucked," Margo said.

"Tell me about it."

"What does it have to say about this?" Margo asked, gesturing toward the black ball.

Jane tossed the Magic 8 to Margo.

"Will our mother ever listen to Jane?" Margo asked. She checked the answer and smiled.

"What? What did it say?" Jane asked.

"I'm sure if you asked it nicely, it would tell you itself."

"But it always works better when you're asking on someone else's behalf."

"You make up the weirdest superstitions, Janie." Margo tossed the ball back.

"Will Margo and Kara get married?" Jane asked.

"Don't even bother with that question. The answer is no."

"Does Kara like Margo?"

Margo looked at her sister threateningly and ran over to her side so she wouldn't lie to her about the ball's answer. Jane flipped it back over before Margo saw it.

"What? What did it say?"

"Ask it yourself," Jane said with a smirk.

Margo grabbed it back. "Is Jane going on a date with Teo tonight?"

Jane's eyes went wide. "Holy crap! I forgot about Teo!"

Chapter 18

JANE WAS WAITING ON HER FRONT STEPS THAT NIGHT WHEN Teo pulled around the corner. She skipped over to the passenger-side door and hopped into the car.

"Hey," Teo said.

"Hey. So what movie are we seeing?" Jane asked as he pulled away from the curb.

Teo looked confused. "I guess we never decided that detail."

"I do this thing where I just go to the movies and see what's playing next. Sometimes I end up seeing a movie I might not have seen otherwise, and it might have more meaning in my life than I could have imagined."

"Sounds like fun," Teo said.

"I like to call it cinematic serendipity. Or at least that's what Margo calls it, since she's the one who named it. I'm the one who had to look up the word *serendipity*."

"But you're the one who made it up," Teo said. "And it's genius."

"I'm really glad you wanted to hang out tonight," Jane said, smiling.

"I don't know why we don't do this more often. It's weird." He stopped there, not wanting to say exactly what he wanted to say—at least not so early in the evening.

"It is weird," Jane said. She didn't say any more, either.

Cinematic serendipity meant that they ended up seeing an action thriller. The plot wasn't bad, but it had way more sex than either of them could have predicted. And not fade-to-black sex. Butts, boobs, and even some side penis. They were both thoroughly embarrassed by it, and their discomfort was only made worse by the main male character's penchant for really loud orgasm noises. Teo couldn't even bring himself to look at Jane.

"Oh my God," Jane gasped as the movie couple started kissing again.

"I guess they feel like they have to take every chance they can, in case it's their last," Teo said in a decent impression of the main character.

"But, like, how do they even do it so much? Don't they get tired after a long day of chasing bad guys?" Jane asked, laughing.

If there had been a lot of other people in the theater with them, they would have totally gotten shushed, but thanks to some bad reviews that Teo and Jane hadn't read and because the movie had already been out for a month, there was only a sprinkling of other people in theater.

"That does not seem like appropriate work wear to me," Teo said.

"I mean, to each his own, but assless chaps in public are so last year," Jane said.

Acknowledging what was happening on-screen made both of them feel less embarrassed about it. Teo kind of hoped that would translate into real life.

"So," Teo said as they were walking out of the movie, "you know how things have been a little, um, awkward between us lately, beyond the obvious dad stuff? Like that time I tried to kiss you and I fell on my face?"

"Yeah," Jane said, glancing over at him as though he was about to pummel her with a truth she didn't want to hear. "I was wondering if we were ever going to talk about that."

"Did that movie make it better or worse?"

Jane stopped in the middle of the sidewalk, and Teo was worried that she was going to run away. But instead he noticed she was laughing so hard she couldn't walk.

"Oh my God," she gasped, putting her hands on her knees.

"So, better?"

"Yeah, you know, I think it did make things better. Perhaps that was the serendipity of it." Jane stood up and smiled, looking across the parking lot. "Is it weird that the movie made me crave frozen yogurt?"

"Maybe a little," Teo said. "But I really want some now, too."

The frozen-yogurt place was bright and cool compared with the parking lot, which still held on to the heat of the day.

"So do you have a theory on fro-yo, too?" Teo asked, bumping his hip playfully into Jane's.

"I have lots of theories."

"But are any of them as awesome as your cinematic serendipity theory?"

"Nothing can beat cinematic serendipity." Jane grabbed a cup and handed one to Teo.

"Well, I have a theory on fro-yo," he said.

"Oh, I cannot wait," Jane said.

"It's all about flavor palate and sticking to it. You could go fruit; you could go chocolate; you could go mixed nuts or cereal. You need to stick to a theme, and you will never be disappointed."

"And I tend to disagree. I like a little bit of everything all mixed together."

"Were you one of those kids who would put all different sodas in the same cup?"

"One of those kids? I am still one of those kids, thank you very much," Jane said, fake indignation in her voice. "What flavor palate are you going for tonight?"

"Maybe nuts for nuts?" Teo said, surveying the flavor choices.

"You could mix some of the pistachio with the chocolate hazelnut."

"Or I could go with cake batter and do most of the flavoring up with the toppings."

"Boring," Jane said.

"Well, what's your plan?"

"Peanut butter and strawberry."

Teo narrowed his eyes, trying to understand the connection.

"Because it's like peanut butter and jelly. Then I'll do a mix of chocolate and fruit and put raspberry syrup on top," Jane explained.

"That actually sounds delicious."

"It will be."

They set to work getting their yogurt and then putting on the toppings.

"But you do realize you've chosen a flavor palate," Teo said.

Jane put a heap of gummy bears and Fruity Pebbles on top just to prove Teo wrong.

"Enjoy your weird mix of textures," he said.

When it was time to pay, Jane grabbed both cups, put them on the scale, and paid for them.

"You didn't have to pay," Teo said.

"I wanted to."

The bench outside was empty, so they sat down and watched the stream of people going in and out of the movie theater.

"There's something I want to talk to you about," Teo said.

Jane gripped her cup tighter and took a deep breath, as if preparing for some kind of major announcement. As if she was living the last moment of her life before everything changed.

Something between them had shifted during the course of the evening, and this moment had to mean that Teo felt it, too.

He touched the back of her hand, and Jane looked up to meet his gaze.

"I want to meet my dad."

Jane's face fell a little bit, but she covered it up with a spoonful of gummy bears.

"Wow," Jane said. "That wasn't exactly what I was expecting."

"Yeah. I don't know what changed."

"This is a big decision. Huge. Epic, even."

"I know."

"I wish I could consult my Magic 8."

"What do you think it would say?"

Jane pretended to hold the ball in her hand. "Should Teo meet Mateo Rodriguez?" She looked over at Teo with a frown. " 'Reply hazy, try again.' "

Teo frowned.

Jane sighed.

"Hypothetically, what would I need to do? To see him?" He glanced at her out of the corner of his eye.

Jane ate a spoonful of her fro-yo and stared into space.

"You're really good at this stuff," Teo continued. "I don't even know where to start, but I feel like you probably do."

"Hmm, I could get contact information for you. Maybe you could write him a letter, explain who you think you might be."

"What if I wanted to go see him?"

"That's . . . one idea."

"One bad idea?"

"There are a lot of things to consider. How would you get

there? Where would you stay? What if we're completely wrong about this guy and he's not related to you in any way whatsoever and he also happens to run a human-trafficking ring?"

"Let's just assume he doesn't."

"Never assume, Teo."

"Come on, Jane," Teo said, his eyes pleading. "I need your help. And I don't think you're wrong. I think you've figured out something that I've spent years working on."

"Maybe," Jane said, shrugging.

"Definitely."

"What if—"

"No, no what-ifs. There are too many what-ifs. I want to make this decision and stick to it. But I need your help to make it a reality. Please?"

Jane couldn't deny his enthusiasm. It was catching.

"Fine," she said, rolling her eyes and smiling.

"So what would it take to make this happen?" he asked.

"Well, first we'd need to check his schedule. I think if you want to show up out of nowhere, maybe showing up after a class makes more sense than showing up at his house. He probably has random kids approaching him all the time at work. You won't seem as threatening."

"Why would I seem threatening?"

"Maybe *threatening* isn't the right word. But some guy showing up at his house claiming to be his son might freak him out."

Teo nodded. "What else?"

"You'd need to decide how you want to get there. I don't know exactly how far away it is, but you could fly there, or maybe take a bus? Or you could drive."

"I've never driven that far. It makes me kind of nervous."

"So driving's out."

Teo nodded.

"We'd need to figure out a lot of stuff. If you flew, how would you get to the airport? How much does a plane ticket cost? That kind of stuff."

"Can teenagers even buy plane tickets?" Teo asked.

"Teenagers can do anything online as long as they have a credit card."

"I have a debit rewards card with a Visa logo."

"Does it have enough money on it to pay for a plane ticket?"

"I have a lot of money. I'm a responsible saver."

"Well then, if you're so independently wealthy, you probably should have paid for the fro-yo."

Teo laughed. "So you'll help me?"

"Yeah. It makes me a little nervous, the way you want to do this, but I'll help you. Of course I'll help. I started this whole mess in the first place."

"It's not a mess."

"It's a mess, just like this bucket of sludge I created. The Fruity Pebbles are dissolving and creating some kind of paste with the gummy bears."

"Mine is delicious. I appreciate the recommendation."

"Maybe you should share yours with me."

"Probably not."

"It was my idea."

"I don't think so." Teo stood up and started walking to the car.

"Friends share food!" Jane yelled.

"Come on, Jane. Let's go home. We have a lot of work to do."

"I think you need to sleep on it," she said, catching up to him.

"I will. I promise. But maybe we can get together soon? To go over some ideas?"

Jane nodded.

Teo thought about kissing her—he really did, especially when he was dropping her off a few minutes later—but he didn't want to cloud the issue. He didn't want her to think he was kissing her as some kind of payment for helping him.

They chatted idly on the way home. Every word she said made him want to kiss her. He couldn't stop watching her mouth.

"What?" she asked, looking at him intently as they pulled up in front of her house.

"Nothing."

"Is it something else about your dad? You can tell me."

He shook his head. When it was time to kiss Jane, he wanted it to be about Jane. He didn't want it getting all mixed up with this dad stuff.

She got out of the car and then paused on the curb. "This was a lot of fun."

"It was," Teo agreed.

As soon as she walked through her front door, waving over her shoulder to him, he leaned his head on the steering wheel.

"I really should have kissed her."

Chapter 19

ON MONDAY, JANE AND TEO TRIED TO DISCUSS THE PLAN, but there wasn't much time and, as Teo pointed out, you never knew when his sisters were listening or what they were absorbing. But over the next couple of days, they managed to add more details to the plan whenever they had a moment without the girls around.

Despite Jane's reservations, Teo's inexplicable optimism triumphed, and before she knew it, she was booking a plane ticket to Champaign, Illinois.

"So there's a flight from Philly to Chicago, and then you change planes and go from Chicago to Champaign."

"How long will it take?"

"Like, five hours if everything goes as planned. It's kind of expensive."

Teo looked at the computer screen. "I don't care. I have the money."

"How do you want to get from the airport to campus?"

"There are different ways?"

"Yes."

"See? This is why I need your help. I never would have thought of that. What are my choices?"

"You could take a shuttle, or we could book a car, or you could hail a cab. Or, you know, there's always the whole getting-in-touch-with-this-guy-and-finding-out-whether-he's-your-dad-before-you-leave. And if he is your dad, I bet he'd be happy to pick you up at the airport."

"I really want the element of surprise on my side."

"Can we talk about how you reacted to the 'surprise' when I told you I found your dad? Do you want to do that to him?"

Teo sighed. "I don't know. It just feels like I should do it this way."

"You realize you could ask your mom. Or just flat-out tell her you found Mateo Rodriguez and you want to know the truth."

"That sounds like the most hellish confrontation I could ever imagine."

"Even as I was saying it, I realized how terrible it would be to live through," Jane said. "When do you want me to schedule the flight back?"

"I don't know. Just book it one way."

Jane looked up at him, her face scared. "It's a lot more expensive if we do that."

Teo shrugged. "I have the money."

"Fine, a one-way ticket for now." Jane couldn't hide how upset that made her, but she wasn't sure Teo had noticed. He was lost in his own thoughts. Jane tapped away at the laptop, unable to ignore her shaking hands. It shouldn't feel like she was sending Teo on a futile mission, but it did.

The topic came up again and again as the trip got closer. It was one long, never ending conversation.

"Whatever you find in Illinois could be a million times worse than anything you could expect," Jane said.

"If this is a pep talk, I need you to know that you're doing it wrong."

"I'm sorry. I'm just worried. My imagination keeps running off in all different directions."

"Like the human-trafficker theory?"

"There's that one. And the more realistic one where things go wrong in one way or another and you end up alone in a strange city with nowhere to stay. You're hungry, it's raining, your cell phone dies."

"Like I'm a stray puppy?"

"Exactly like that," Jane said, patting his head. "A stray puppy with a dead cell phone."

"I really do appreciate your concern. And I promise I won't sit hungry in the rain."

"You definitely won't, because I have a contingency plan for you," she said, pulling a folded scrap of paper out of her pocket.

Teo flipped it open and looked at it.

"That's the phone number of one of my fandom friends. Her name's Mindy. She lives off campus and said you could give her a call if something went wrong."

"How do you have friends in Illinois?" Teo asked.

"I told you, fandom."

"I don't understand."

"It doesn't matter. But you can call that number anytime— she knows about you. I bet she could even help you book a flight home if you're worried about that."

He put the piece of paper in his wallet. "Thanks, Jane."

"I had to make sure you had a fail-safe. And don't forget about the time difference."

"I totally would have forgotten about the time difference."

"It's going to work in your favor on the way to Illinois, so you should easily get there before his class ends at three o'clock."

"I'm going to do this," Teo said to himself as much as to Jane.

"You are."

A few hours later, Teo whispered a question to Jane as she cleaned up from lunch.

"How do I get to the airport on Wednesday morning?"

"I'll drive you to the bus stop at, like, four thirty. There's a superearly bus to Philly that stops a couple of miles from here."

"How did you figure that out so fast?"

"Because I knew you would need to get to the airport," Jane said. "It's all logic, Teo. If you sat down and thought about it, you would have gotten there eventually."

"You're awesome," he said.

"Thanks."

The twenty-four hours leading up to Teo's departure seemed to drag on forever. Jane didn't sleep at all Tuesday night, instead tossing and turning and thinking about what Teo was about to do.

Around four o'clock on Wednesday morning, she got out of bed and dressed quickly. She sat down with her trusty Magic 8.

"Will Teo be okay?" she asked.

Most likely.

"Will Teo be better than okay?"

Cannot predict now.

That was definitely not the answer she was looking for, but there was no time to ask more questions. No matter how she felt about this trip, she couldn't be late picking up Teo. She slipped out of the house and prayed that no one would notice she was gone.

The sound of her car starting seemed like an atomic bomb going off in the quiet predawn hours. She pulled around the corner and found Teo waiting on the curb.

"Morning," Teo said, getting into Jane's car.

"That's a lie." Jane yawned. "If it was morning, the sun would be up."

They drove through empty streets to the bus shelter on the other side of town. Jane parked the car and waited with Teo.

"Thank you again for the millionth time," Teo said.

Jane smirked. "Just make sure you read all the signs going through the security lines at the airport. Do you have your ID?"

"Yes." He wiped his palms on his shorts. "I also left my mom a note saying my car wouldn't start this morning and I had someone from work pick me up super early because we were going out for breakfast before active-adult water yoga."

"Okay, good to know."

"That means the minivan is blocked in, but that should help you. If the girls go to the pool today, they'll notice I'm not there, and it'll totally blow my cover."

"What if your mom or Buck tries to start your car this morning?"

"They won't. Mornings are too hectic. They won't try until tonight."

"Are you going to talk to them at all?"

"I think I'll call later or in the morning, depending on how I'm feeling about everything."

"Let's go over the plan one more time," Jane said.

"We know Mateo Rodriguez will be in his office on Wednesday afternoon for office hours. I took today, tomorrow, and Friday off from work. My mom probably won't notice I'm gone until late tomorrow night. I could even tell her I'm staying at someone's house for a couple of days. I could be gone almost the whole time before she would notice."

"Good."

"I have your friend Mindy's phone number. And if worst comes to worst, I could take a bus to Chicago that runs every few hours from campus, then wait at the airport until I can get a flight home."

"I really hope nothing goes wrong," Jane said.

"Nothing's going to go wrong," Teo said, rubbing her arm. "You planned it down to the minute."

"I feel like I should be the one reassuring you."

"No way. I am totally confident in you and your plan."

The bus came into view then, stopped at a light two blocks away. Jane and Teo stood.

"Even if I'm not entirely confident in the plan, I swear I support this endeavor and will do whatever you need me to do on this end," Jane said.

"You have no idea how much that means to me."

They smiled at each other.

As the bus pulled up, Jane felt a rush of panic. She handed Teo all the money in her pocket. "I know it's only, like, ten bucks, but have breakfast at the airport on me."

"Okay," he said.

"And please let me know that you're alive and safe when you get there."

"I promise."

"All right. Please be careful. And I don't mean just with the traveling but also with yourself. Take care of yourself."

"I will."

"And—"

"Jane, come on, I gotta go." The bus driver was staring at them.

Jane stepped onto her tiptoes and hugged him tightly, as if she could hug all her feelings and good luck and hope into him if she could squeeze him hard enough.

He squeezed back.

"Bye," he said, drawing away.

"Good luck!" she said.

He took the seat closest to the front and waved as the bus pulled away.

Jane watched it until she could no longer see it.

She sat down on the bench in the bus shelter, trying to sort out her emotions.

She wished she had kissed him. But kissing him would have opened up a whole can of worms that she wasn't prepared to deal with at 4:48 in the morning. Not to mention that she wouldn't want Teo to have to deal with that kind of crap at this moment, either.

Except that her feelings weren't crap. They were growing every day, and this trip, and the way she felt about it, only cemented them for her.

She knew she needed to get home before anyone noticed her absence, but each of her limbs felt like it weighed a thousand pounds, and her brain was clouded with worry. She sat on the bench a little longer.

It was only when she was walking back to her car that she realized she was crying. She could only hope that Teo knew what he was getting himself into.

Jane wiped at the tears with the hem of her T-shirt and drove home.

Chapter 20

WITHIN A MINUTE AFTER THE BUS LEFT THE CURB, TEO HAD to stop himself from leaping out of the seat and telling the driver to let him get off.

There weren't very many people on the bus at this time of the morning, and Teo had chosen the seat closest to the driver because the idea of walking much farther down the aisle wasn't appealing. But now he was sitting on his hands like a child whose mother had yelled at him, just trying to keep himself from jumping out the emergency exit.

He could envision the scene if he leaped up and started yelling. The driver's shocked expression, his fellow passengers' faces etched with confusion, the relief he would feel running back down the street to Jane.

In fact, this vision was probably Jane's fault. Her

imagination was rubbing off on him.

But he kept himself together, making it to the airport. He started to sweat when he tried to check in at a ticket kiosk and the screen kept saying that his confirmation number was invalid. It took two more tries before he realized he was trying to check in with the wrong airline.

Things went more smoothly after that, even if the whole thing was overwhelming. He tried to take it one step at a time. He found the gate and waited to board. He located his seat and stowed his carry-on properly under the seat in front of him. He gripped the arms of the chair during takeoff and listened to the same five songs on repeat during the whole flight because he didn't feel like finding a new playlist on his phone.

The shuttle was waiting right where Jane told him it would be, and he was on campus in no time. He texted Jane to tell her he was okay and then put his phone on silent. He needed to do this himself.

It was a quiet Wednesday afternoon on campus. He wondered if all campuses were like this in the summer. If they were, it wasn't a shock that his mom would rather spend her time doing work in the campus library than at home with his three screaming little sisters.

When he found the right building, he checked the time on his phone and saw a string of text messages from Jane. He didn't even let the words sink in before slipping the phone back into his pocket.

He walked through the main doors and followed the

directions Jane had gotten online.

Thoughts of Jane helped him make his way through the halls and up a flight of stairs until he found himself in front of a door that read MATEO RODRIGUEZ.

All he had to do was knock.

JANE WAS IN THE MIDST OF THE LONGEST DAY OF HER LIFE.

When she got to work that morning, Connie showed her the note Teo had left. Jane read it with bleary eyes, even though she already knew the contents.

"I don't have time to deal with his car this morning," Connie said. "So that means it will be in the way all day."

"That's okay. I'll find other stuff to do with the girls around the house."

Connie squeezed her shoulder. "Thank you, Jane. You've been a real asset this summer."

"It's been a great time," Jane said, and she wasn't lying.

Connie left, and the girls came tumbling into the kitchen dressed in what Jane could only describe as bathing costumes.

Each one was wearing a normal bathing suit, but with leis and straw skirts, and Keegan had on something that was probably supposed to be a sarong but looked more like a toga. Because she was seven.

"We're going to have a fashion show," Keegan told Jane.

"Do I get to watch?" Jane asked.

"Yes!" Piper said, taking Jane's hand and leading her to the couch. "You sit here and clap for each of our outfits."

"I can handle that," Jane said, settling in for what she hoped would be a full morning of entertainment for the girls. Unfortunately, they tired of it when Rory almost choked herself trying to get her bathing suit off over her head.

It didn't help that Jane was a terrible combination of emotions, and the girls could probably sense her unrest. She was tapping her fingers on any surface she could find and running her hands through her hair, and yawns overtook every other sentence she spoke.

After the near disaster with the bathing suit, Jane persuaded the girls to spend the rest of the morning watching a movie while she snuggled into the corner of the sectional and dozed on and off. It wasn't her most professional decision, but she was beat.

The girls were pulling her from every direction when it was lunchtime. Jane was sleepwalking by that point, making their peanut butter and jelly sandwiches on autopilot. Thank God they hadn't wanted soup and grilled cheese, because there was a good chance she would have burned the house down.

She checked her cell phone again and again, without finding any messages from Teo. If his flight ran even a few minutes late, he could lose his window of opportunity. He would have to track Mateo Rodriguez down after office hours, and that could get a little complicated. Jane kept her fingers crossed, in between the tapping and hair touching, because there was nothing else for her to do.

"We want to go to the pool!" Keegan said after lunch. She really was like the union president when it came to her sisters.

Aside from the fact Teo wouldn't be at the pool and she had no way to get them there, Jane couldn't imagine having to watch them in the water this afternoon. Even after slugging two cups of coffee with lots of flavored creamer, she still wasn't at her most energetic.

Jane did the only thing she could think of: She finally made good on her promise to create an at-home sprayground.

The girls walked with Jane to her house and helped bring back the Slip 'N Slide. They set it up in the front yard, along with the sprinkler and the baby pool.

Jane turned on the lawn sprinklers, and the girls were thrilled. Jane sat on the steps and watched them run around and slip and dance and be silly for a solid thirty minutes.

Around two o'clock, Jane got a text from Teo. He said he was in Champaign and he'd get in touch with her when he knew more. She texted him back.

Jane

I'm glad you're okay!

You can do this.

Just focus on why you're there.

♥ 195 ♥

> I know I wasn't really all rah-rah this morning, but I'm happy you're doing this.

> I'm happy for you.

> Treat him like a Magic 8 if you need to. ☺

EIGHT HUNDRED MILES AWAY, TEO WAS QUIETLY PANICKING.

He paced the unfamiliar hallway and cracked his knuckles. And then, miraculously, the door swung open and there stood Mateo Rodriguez.

"Hello there."

An odd sort of discouragement flooded every bone in Teo's body. He hadn't acknowledged the thought previously, but he had hoped deep down inside that his father would recognize him as soon as he saw his face. That wasn't the case.

Teo swallowed.

"Are you in one of my classes? Or are you signing up? Cat got your tongue?"

Teo shook his head.

"Do you want to come in for office hours?" Mateo asked, gesturing for Teo to walk through the door. Teo followed him. He felt like he was in a trance, as if he'd been hypnotized and no one remembered the magic word to wake him up.

"Are you okay?" Mateo asked when Teo stood uncomfortably

next to a chair. "You look like you might be ill."

Teo did feel like he might be ill. Every strand of hair on his body stood at attention, and sweat trickled down his forehead. He fought the urge to crack his knuckles again, but lost and ended up cracking every finger individually.

"Is there something I can help you with?" Mateo Rodriguez asked. Teo could hear the way his voice was getting worried, the way it pitched up at the end of the question. Teo looked at the man across from him, taking in the graying temples and icy-blue metal of his glasses. Teo liked him. He just wished that the man across the desk recognized his long lost-son.

Teo stood up to leave. Obviously something was wrong with him—he couldn't speak in front of the man he'd come all this way to see. His phone slipped out of his pocket and landed on the floor, waking itself up. All Jane's texts were lit up on the screen, and he read them quickly, the last one really standing out.

Jane

Treat him like a Magic 8 if you need to. ☺

And that was what woke him up. He could ask yes-or-no questions. He could manage that, to bring the truth out slowly.

"Do you know who I am?" Teo asked.

"No."

"Do you know Connie Garcia?"

Mateo smiled fondly. "I do."

"Did you know she had a son?"

♥ *197* ♥

"I did not know that." He rubbed his chin. "Are you her son?"

Teo nodded, knocked slightly off balance by having to answer a question himself.

"Are you thinking about coming here for school? Did Connie send you? I didn't know she knew I worked here."

Teo shook his head this time.

"Then why—" Mateo started.

"My name is Teo Garcia, and I think I might be your son," Teo said, interrupting.

"Oh."

Chapter 21

JANE CHEWED HER NAILS DOWN TO THE QUICK, WAITING AND waiting for more information from Teo. At least she knew he'd gotten there and he hadn't been killed or kidnapped. Knowing he was alive and okay made her heart stop slamming around in her chest.

Unless his kidnapper had used Teo's phone to text Jane and give her a false sense of comfort. They would have to make a Lifetime original movie about this. She spent a few minutes thinking of titles for it, finally settling on *Taken at the Airport: The Teo Garcia Story*.

She sent another text about an hour after getting his message:

> **Text random numbers if you've been kidnapped.**

> **That is, if your kidnapper is even letting you hold on to your phone.**

When Connie got home an hour earlier than usual, the girls were still playing in the baby pool, even though Jane had made them turn off the sprinkler earlier.

"Hi, Mommy!" they yelled.

Connie waved at them and took a seat next to Jane on the steps.

"I apologize if your water bill is astronomical next month," Jane said.

Connie laughed. "They look very happy, so I imagine it'll be worth it."

"Yeah, they're in great moods today."

"I wish my son could be in half as good a mood as these three are. I never see him smile anymore."

Jane hummed in response. She saw him smile all the time, but she didn't want to make Connie feel bad.

"He grunts answers and seems unhappy with everything," Connie went on. "I don't look forward to him coming home later, angry about his car not starting and acting like it's somehow my fault. Or Buck's fault. Lately, a lot of things—at least according to Teo—are Buck's fault."

Jane tried to think of something to say to make Connie feel better. But she knew too much now. She knew too much about what was going on behind the scenes in the Garcia-Buchanan household, and she was too aware that Connie could have fixed her relationship with Teo a long time ago. Maybe not fixed it, but at least made it better somehow. Talked to him about his father instead of ignoring the issue. But it wasn't Jane's place to say that.

"Has he said anything to you?" Connie asked.

Jane opened her mouth, taking a deep breath, hoping that maybe a bug would fly in and keep her from having to answer Connie's question. But there were no kamikaze bugs that day.

"I don't know," Jane said. "I feel like he's been sad about something, but I don't know what. We're not really that close." Except they were close enough that Jane had driven him to the bus stop before dawn so he could fly away and find his father. She wasn't sure you could really get much closer than that.

"I don't want to put you on the spot, Jane. I thought maybe he mentioned something. I know part of the problem is that Ravi has been gone all summer long and Teo hasn't had an outlet. But he seemed to be talking to you more. The girls even mentioned it."

Jane looked over at the three girls splashing in the baby pool. "They're very observant."

"Do you think he's okay?"

"He's fine," Jane said, even though every minute that ticked by made her think that maybe he really had been kidnapped.

"It's weird that he left that note this morning. It solidified all these worries I've had about him pulling away. Like he's going to be the kind of person who goes away to college and never comes home again. I don't want that for him."

"What does Buck say?" Jane asked. It was an odd question, but it was something she often wondered about. Buck's opinion of Teo was a complete mystery to her.

"Buck says it'll be fine. He says Teo's been getting better lately, not worse. I think Buck's a little bit in denial."

Jane nodded. "I think every family has problems like this as the kids grow up. I know my parents are kind of dealing with it right now."

"Thank you for listening, Janie," Connie said, giving Jane's shoulder a squeeze.

"Not a problem," Jane said.

"Anything you need to discuss, now that I've talked your ear off with my troubles?"

Jane wished she could. She wanted to spill everything to Connie, sitting there in the afternoon sun with the girls dancing around the lawn and the cicadas chirping in the trees. She would tell Connie that she didn't want to go to college and that she didn't know what to do about Teo. She would tell her that right that very second Teo was in Illinois meeting his father. Jane would tell Connie everything. But too much of it wasn't hers to tell, and the thought of trying to talk about college and the future just made her more exhausted.

"I'm good," Jane said.

"You look tired."

"Just staying up too late, watching TV and chatting on the Internet."

Connie smiled. "You know where to find me if you ever need me."

"I do," Jane said.

On her way home, she sent another string of text messages. It wasn't enough to know that Teo hadn't been kidnapped; she needed to know he was okay.

AFTER TEO DECLARED HIS PARENTAGE, THE OFFICE GREW very, very quiet. Mateo sat behind his desk with his hands clasped, and his jaw dropped slightly.

Teo held his breath, his fight-or-flight response once more telling him emphatically to flee, to run all the way back to New Jersey.

"I think I need a coffee. Would you like to join me?" Mateo asked.

"Um, sure," Teo said.

They walked to the student center in silence. When they got there, Mateo offered to buy Teo a drink, too.

"Water would be fine," Teo said. He sat at a table and waited while Mateo ordered coffee and purchased a bottle of water.

When Teo took a second to check his phone, he found a string of text messages from Jane about being kidnapped.

Jane

Text random numbers if you've been kidnapped.

That is, if your kidnapper is even letting you hold on to your phone.

The more I think about this subject, the more I realize that the kidnapper would have tossed your phone into a river.

They wouldn't want anyone to be able to track you/ them.

It's been a long time, Teo.

I just need to know you're alive.

Hellllllloooooooooooooooooo

I don't know what the going rate is for a young, handsome devil like yourself on the black market, but I'm sure it's high.

Where is the black market, anyway?

Could I find it?

Please just answer me, Teo. Please tell me you're okay. I know you arrived, but I want to know if you've found him yet, if you have a place to sleep tonight.

All right. Fine.

Two can play at this game.

This is my final text.

Just remember to get in touch with Mindy if you need to.

Now I'm not joking anymore. THIS is my final text.

Teo couldn't help smiling. It was all so very Jane.

Teo

I'm fine. We're getting coffee. I'll text later.

She responded immediately, and he could hear her voice saying the words.

♥ 205 ♥

THANK GOD YOU'RE ALIVE.

Mateo sat down across from Teo then and handed him the bottle of water.

"I think you might have me confused with my brother, Jose."

"Oh," Teo said. "Yeah. That's a possibility. That's the name that showed up on my birth certificate. But my friend Jane found you, and we couldn't find him."

Mateo nodded. "I'm sorry to be the one to have to tell you this, but Jose died about fifteen years ago."

Teo felt the air go out of him. In all their talk of contingencies, possibilities, and the various ways things could go wrong, they'd never considered that Teo's dad could be dead.

"I'm very sorry," Mateo said.

Teo shook his head.

"He was young. He had just gotten out of the air force. I wrote Connie to tell her, even. They hadn't spoken in years."

Teo couldn't stop shaking his head. This time, he didn't think he'd be able to control his fight-or-flight.

"I don't think he knew about you," Mateo added.

A tear trailed down Teo's cheek. That was exactly what he needed to hear. That was the good news in all this. And that was what kept him from running.

But even as he felt relief about his father, the anger that had been growing all summer toward his mother finally erupted.

"She never told him about me?" he asked.

"Not that I know of. Jose wasn't much for keeping secrets. I think if he'd known, he would have told me."

"She never—" Teo said, shaking his head. A feeling of betrayal flooded his brain. All that time, all those years, she'd never told anyone about Teo, like he was a shameful secret. Like he was something to hide. Teo's hands tightened into fists, and he could hardly keep himself from punching the wall.

"Hey, hey," Mateo said, holding his hands up defensively.

"No, it's okay. I'm sorry. I can't believe she never told my father."

"What are you doing here, kid?"

"I came looking for you."

"Does Connie know where you are?"

"Um, yes."

His uncle—he had an uncle, a real blood-related uncle, not one of those impostors from Buck's family—looked at him doubtfully but didn't challenge him.

"How did you get here?"

"Plane," Teo said.

Mateo rubbed at his eyes and then slugged down the rest of his coffee. "Why don't you come back to my place? It's a couple of blocks from here. We should talk this out a little more. And I should probably call your mom."

♥ *207* ♥

"Yeah, sure. But I'll call my mom, okay? You don't have to do that."

Mateo nodded.

When they got to Mateo's condo, Teo sent Jane a long text.

Teo

I'm not coming home. Mateo's my uncle, not my dad. My dad's dead. I don't want to talk to my mom. I don't want to deal with her lies. I'm just going to stay here. If Mateo won't let me stay with him, I'll figure it out. Just don't worry about me. I'll come up with a plan. Thanks for all your help.

Then he turned off his phone and sat down with his uncle.

Chapter 22

Jane read and reread Teo's latest text. She had sent multiple responses to it last night, but he was obviously ignoring her. (Or he'd been kidnapped. She still didn't want to rule out a kidnapping.) She had even tried calling him.

Now it was morning, and she was at the Buchanans', and there wasn't a heck of a lot she could do about Teo at the moment. But she couldn't stop thinking about him. Even though it was her last day of babysitting, she couldn't give the girls her full attention.

There was something about the tone of Teo's text that made Jane want to see him immediately, to look him in the eye and talk some sense into him. He loved to tell her how logical she was. Maybe it was time to really show off her logic and make an impression.

But how?

She was stuck, at least until Connie got back from class.

Connie had promised she wouldn't be gone long, and she made good on that promise, arriving home just before eleven.

"I want to make sure I'm here when Teo gets back from work," she explained. "I only needed to drop off a paper on campus. I can take care of the rest of my finals online."

"Do you want me to stay and watch the girls while you work?" Jane asked, even though she wanted nothing more than to go home immediately.

"No, it's fine. You go ahead. I'll pay you for the rest of the day."

"Thanks, Connie," Jane said, looking at her last paycheck. It looked like Connie had added more than the rest of the afternoon.

"You were wonderful this summer, Jane." Connie leaned over to give her an extra-long hug, and Jane felt a sharp sting of guilt for not telling her where Teo really was.

Jane said good-bye to Keegan, Rory, and Piper and promised that she would see them all the time—that even though she wouldn't see them every day, they still lived in the same neighborhood.

"We'll have Jane come babysit again soon, okay, girls?" Connie said when all three of them got a little teary-eyed. Even Jane got emotional looking at their little quivering chins.

After a few more hugs, Jane walked out the front door and nearly ran headfirst into none other than Ravi Singh.

"Oh. Shit."

"Lovely to see you, too, Jane," Ravi said. "Now, if you'll kindly remove yourself from the center of the walk, I would like to go visit with my dear friend Teo."

"When was the last time you talked to him?" Jane asked.

"Well, not that it's any of your business, but I would say a week ago. Before I knew I was coming home."

"He's not here," Jane said, shaking her head. "He's gone."

"Gone? Where?"

"It's a long story."

"It's a long story that you know and I don't?" Ravi asked, completely mystified by the concept. "I guess that's what I get for spending the past forty-eight hours sleeping off my jet lag. I woke up in bizarro world."

"Okay, we need to talk," Jane said, pulling on Ravi's arm.

"I don't think so." He moved out of her grip.

"Please. Just come home with me. I'll explain everything. But if you go inside, you could potentially mess up the whole plan."

"Me? When have I ever messed anything up? You're the person who messes things up."

"Not this time," Jane said.

"I am a perfect, genius angel who never does anything wrong," Ravi said, talking over her.

"You like Teo, right? He's your best friend."

"Obviously."

"Then come with me and I'll tell you everything, but if you go in there and talk to Connie, the situation could blow up in

Teo's face. And my face. And maybe even your face if I could find a way to get you implicated in the whole thing. Mostly because it would be fun to take you down with us."

"Is this about his dad?"

Jane nodded.

Ravi followed Jane down the street, around the corner, and to her house. She was closing in on a plan but had a few more things to figure out first.

"Margo, thank God you're here," Jane said, pulling Ravi through the front door and into the living room, where they found Margo reading on the couch. "Wait, why are you here?"

"My internship ended last week, but you've had your head in the clouds since your date with Teo, so I'm not exactly shocked you didn't notice."

"Whoa, whoa, whoa," Ravi said. "You're dating Teo? This is the kind of crap that happens when I'm not around to regulate."

"We are not dating," Jane said to Ravi. "It was not a date."

"Then why have you had your head up your ass?" Ravi asked.

"I haven't!"

"I'm quoting your sister."

"My sister doesn't know everything."

"So what's up, then?" Ravi asked. "And where's Teo?"

"Teo's missing?" Margo asked.

"Would you two stop and let me explain what's going on?" Jane said. "Is anyone else home?"

Margo shook her head and put her book down while Ravi took a seat in the armchair and Jane perched on the couch.

"Teo's in Illinois," she explained. "With his uncle. As in, his dad's brother."

"Is his dad there?" Margo asked. "I thought he was looking for his dad."

"His dad is dead," Jane said.

"Poor Teo," Margo and Ravi said in unison.

"It sucks, right? I feel so responsible because I'm the one who started all this in the first place."

"He didn't have to go, Jane," Ravi said.

"You know it must be true if Ravi's comforting you," Margo said.

Ravi looked startled. "I didn't mean that. It's all your fault."

Jane rolled her eyes. "The problem is that now he's talking about not coming home. And I need your help," Jane said, addressing Margo.

"I'll do anything," Ravi said.

"I don't really need your help."

"I volunteer as tribute!" he said, standing up.

Jane ignored him and turned back to Margo. "I'm going to find him. I need to see him, to talk to him. I feel like he's confused right now and has no clue what he's even saying. Like he's just making rash decisions to piss off his mom."

"Are you sure he wasn't exaggerating about staying?"

"That's possible, but I don't really want to chance it."

"What the heck are we waiting for?" Ravi asked, clapping his hands. "Let's go."

Jane rubbed her face with her hands and sighed. "No," she said simply.

"If you don't let me go with you, I'm totally going to ruin your plan."

"Grow up, Ravi," Jane said.

He deflated. "I'm serious. My bro needs me. I need to be there."

"Do you have any money?" Jane asked.

"Oh, so now you're extorting me?"

"No, we're all going to put money in."

"All? What do you mean by *all*?" Margo asked.

"I need you to come, too?" Jane said, her voice rising into a question even though she meant to make a statement.

"Seriously? Mom and Dad are going to be so pissed."

"They're not going to be that pissed at you. They're going to be really pissed at me, but I need your help. You can't rent a hotel room if you're under eighteen, and there's no way we're going to be able to do a twenty-six-hour round trip without at least a couple of hours of sleep."

"Sleep in the car," Margo suggested.

"Come on, Margo, please?"

"I don't know."

"You won't have to put in any money," Jane said.

"Hey, if she doesn't have to put in any money, I don't know why I have to put in any money," Ravi said.

Then, "Fine, I'll go. When are we leaving?"

"In like ten minutes? After I pack a couple things?"

Jane and Margo ran up the stairs, leaving Ravi to wander

around the house. Jane hoped he wouldn't start going through photo albums. She didn't need Ravi to find the pictures of her taking a bath as a toddler.

Jane looked around her room, trying to decide what she needed. Phone charger, underwear, a change of clothes, deodorant, hairbrush, and toothbrush were all definites. Something pretty to wear when she surprised Teo? It couldn't hurt. She tossed it all into a duffel bag and was ready to hit the road.

At the last second, she looked at her Magic 8 Ball.

"Am I doing the right thing?" she asked it.

It is certain.

"Should I bring you with me?"

She didn't even wait for an answer before tossing the ball into her bag.

"I'm driving," Ravi said when Jane rejoined him downstairs in the living room. He was lounging on the couch, reading a copy of *Real Simple* magazine.

"Hell, no," Margo said, coming down the stairs behind Jane. "We'll follow you home to drop off your car and grab whatever you might need overnight, but Jane's driving. She's in charge."

"Thanks, Margo," Jane said.

"You're welcome."

"Jane drives garbage on wheels," Ravi said, rolling up *Real Simple* and taking it with him as they left.

"Are you really stealing our mother's magazine?" Margo asked.

"It has some great gift ideas for under twenty-five dollars. And since I'm going to be using all my money on the great Jane caper, I might as well find something inexpensive yet tasteful to get my mom for her birthday next month."

"You're ridiculous," Margo said. "You are a ridiculous human being."

"I take that as a compliment," Ravi said.

"All right, let's get going before Mom comes home and realizes that we have overnight bags with us."

"Did you leave her a note?" Margo asked.

"No, did you?"

"No."

"Damn. We need to think of something to say."

"Oh, for the love of God," Ravi said. "Just tell her you're going to some kind of girly party or some shit, and let's get out of here. I'm so tired of waiting around for you two."

Both Jane and Margo gave him a death glare.

"Be waiting for us outside your house in fifteen minutes," Margo said.

"How do you know where I live?" Ravi asked, narrowing his eyes.

"Because I went to your birthday party every year from fifth to seventh grade. It's not that hard to find."

"Fine. I'll see you soon. But you'd better not ditch me!" he called as he walked around the corner to get his car.

"He is the worst!" Margo said.

"I've been telling you."

Margo shook her head.

"Concentrate," Jane said. "We need a note for Mom. Then we'll pick up the pain in the ass and go rescue Teo."

"I'm pretty sure he doesn't exactly need rescuing."

"Oh, you know what I mean."

"How's this sound?" Margo asked, showing Jane the note.

"I'm not sure that she's going to believe that we're outlet shopping and sleeping at Claudia's later, but your penmanship is impressive."

"It's the best I can do!"

"I know. We'll just have to hope that she believes we're bonding."

Chapter 23

BY THE TIME JANE AND MARGO PICKED RAVI UP AND GOT ON the road, it was going on one o'clock.

"What took you guys so long?" he whined, getting into the car.

"It literally took us fourteen minutes. One fewer than we promised," Jane said.

"Hmph," was all Ravi said in response.

"According to the traffic app, we'll get there in about thirteen hours," Margo said as they merged onto the highway.

"Do we even know his uncle's address?" Ravi asked.

"No, but we know Mateo's class schedule. We just need to be on campus between ten and twelve tomorrow, while his class is in session, and I'm sure he'll tell us where Teo is once we explain ourselves."

"Or we could text him and ask for the address," Ravi said.

"I think we need the element of surprise on our side," Jane said.

"You sound like Teo," Ravi said. "He's always talking about the element of surprise."

"That's where I got it from," Jane said.

"Why would we want to surprise him?" Margo asked.

"The way I see it, if he knows we're on our way, he's going to be thinking of ways to talk us out of talking him out of staying in Illinois."

"Your sentence structure is overly complex," Ravi said. "But I get the gist of what you're trying to explain."

"Thanks," Jane said, rolling her eyes. "I don't want him to anticipate our arrival and have too much time to think it over. He's going to act like he has options, but the only real option is coming home with us." Jane paused. "There's also the fact that either his phone is off or he's completely ignoring the whole world."

They made it about two hours before they needed to stop to use the restrooms and pick up road snacks.

After that, they went another two hours before they hit traffic. Big-time, rush-hour, construction-zone, stopped-dead traffic.

"This is terrible. Why did you let the GPS take us this way, Jane?"

"Shut up, Ravi," Margo said. "For starters, I'm the navigator. And this was definitely the best option."

Ravi sat back and crossed his arms while the car inched along.

"I think I saw a snail pass us," Ravi complained.

Traffic broke up three miles and forty-five minutes later. They were finally zooming through Pennsylvania at a decent clip.

"I'm starving," Margo announced. "We should stop for dinner soon. And then we can switch, and I'll drive for a while. You need a break."

"No way, Margo. We can't stop again already. We need to make up time from rush hour," Jane said. "At this rate, we'll never get there. And I'm not sure I'm tired enough to put my life in your hands."

"But I'm so hungry," Margo whined.

"Eat more beef jerky. We'll stop when we get closer," Jane said. "Or when one of us has to pee."

"You're mean."

"I have to pee!" Ravi yelled.

Jane glanced at him in the rearview mirror. "Since when are you on Margo's side?"

"I'm not on anyone's side. It's mostly about not being on your side. I saw an opening, so I took it."

Jane eventually let them stop for dinner at McDonald's, and they took a few minutes to discuss their next move.

"According to the GPS, we're not going to get there until three in the morning," Jane said.

"There's no point showing up in the middle of the night," Margo said. "It's not like this guy is holding Teo hostage."

"Do we really know that, though?" Ravi asked. "I bet you didn't even do a background check on him. You sent Teo off to his doom all by himself. How dare you, madam!"

"Are you done now?" Jane asked Ravi.

"Yeah, fine."

She turned back to Margo. "Basically, what you're saying is you think we should stop for the night?" Jane asked.

"Yes," Margo said.

"How are we going to rent a hotel room? Don't you need to be, like, twenty-one?" Ravi asked.

"You only need to be eighteen most places. Although they'll think we're trying to have a hotel party, so you guys are going to have to let me go in by myself."

"You're going to make me sit in the car with Jane the Pain all by myself?"

Jane and Margo glared at Ravi.

"Anyway, I know I can rent a room."

"Won't they think it's weird that you're alone? Like, some young girl in the middle of the night renting a hotel room?"

Margo shrugged. "I'll come up with an excuse just in case and drop it in conversationally if I have to."

"The first place we pass with outside hallways, we'll try," Jane said. "That way you can say you're traveling for business by yourself, rather than try to get anyone to believe that Ravi and I are your children."

"Jane is so obviously adopted," Ravi said.

After they finished eating, they got back out to the car.

"I'll drive," Margo said, and Jane, tired of driving, reluctantly tossed her the keys.

"Shotgun!" Ravi said.

"There's no way I'm sitting in the backseat of my own car."

"Children, children," Margo said, holding up her hands. "Please stop arguing or, so help me, I will turn this car around."

Jane slid into the passenger seat before Ravi even knew what hit him, and they set off.

"So, Ravi, I've been dying to ask: Why do you hate my sister so vehemently?"

"What a great question, Margo. Thank you for asking. No one ever asks."

Margo smiled at the praise.

"Allow me to set the stage for you. Jane and I were in seventh grade. We very rarely ever have classes together, due to my superior intellect, but we ended up in the same science class that year. And one day when our teacher assigned a project, both of our lab partners were absent. So I got stuck with her."

Jane rolled her eyes so many times in a row she started to feel carsick. "How about you drop the dramatics and get to your point?"

Ravi poked his head between the front seats.

"We got a B on our diorama."

"Oh, yeah," Jane said, smiling. "We did. I remember that. It was a diorama of the Amazonian ecosystem."

"We got a B," Ravi repeated.

"I know. It was great."

Ravi blinked at her, stunned. "It was the first B I ever got."

"What?" Margo asked, turning to look at him and jerking the steering wheel.

"Margo! Eyes on the road! You promised," Jane said.

"Fine, fine," Margo said. "That's a tough cherry to pop, though, Ravi. I totally understand. I remember my first B. The horror, the long-lasting sting of mediocrity."

"I forgot I was in the car with geniuses," Jane said. "I live a B lifestyle. More like a C lifestyle, if I'm being honest with myself. They're not actually all that scarring."

But Margo and Ravi weren't listening. Instead, they were bonding over their very rare bad grades.

"I got a D on a paper in my logic class in freshmen year. Can you believe that?"

"I can't," Ravi said. "I'm not sure I could deal."

"The professor let me write another one and averaged the grades. Even then it was only a B minus."

Ravi was shaking his head, and Jane was doing her best not to scream.

"Wait a second! Are you the person who wrote 'Jane Connelly is a B' on my locker in eighth grade?"

"Yes. I hadn't gotten past the sting."

Margo was laughing.

"Don't laugh," Jane said to her. "It was traumatizing. I thought someone was making fun of my boobs or calling me a bitch but the marker ran out of ink."

"Looking back, it's funny," Ravi said.

"You are the worst," Jane said.

Around the Illinois border, Margo pulled the car into the large parking lot of a motel and parked around the corner from the front-desk area. She looked less than confident as she went in, but she was skipping by the time she came out.

"It worked! I told the lady at the desk I was stuck in traffic all day while driving home from dropping my boyfriend off at college, and I just needed somewhere to crash. And she bought it. Lying makes me feel alive!" Margo said.

Jane laughed as she pulled her bag out of the trunk.

"The only thing she said is that checkout is at noon."

"I can imagine how ridiculous you were when you lied to that woman."

"No way! I was amazing. I was like a villain in a movie. I was freaking Keyser Söze."

"I don't know who that is," Jane said.

"You've never seen *The Usual Suspects*?" Ravi asked as they walked across the parking lot toward their room on the first floor.

"I have not," Jane said.

"What is this world coming to?" Ravi asked the night sky, shaking his head.

Margo unlocked the motel room door. "Welcome home, children," she said, swinging it open.

"There's only one bed," Ravi said. "Have you lured me here to take advantage of me? Is that what this is all about? Has this all been a farce? Where is Teo, really?"

"Yes, Ravi. Your self-proclaimed archnemesis and I have lured you to the Illinois border to ravish you. You asshole."

"You're going to ravage my asshole?" Ravi asked, putting his hands on his butt.

"You're a ridiculous human being," Jane said.

"I guess the lady at the desk figured I'd only need a king-size bed, since I'm only one person. We'll have to share. It's a huge freaking bed," Margo said.

Jane pulled the bedspread off and threw it onto one of the armchairs. "I hate thinking about all the other people who have slept here."

"You and *Dateline*," Margo mumbled.

"There's no way I'm sharing a bed with you two," Ravi said. "You'll both have to sleep on the floor."

"Oh, come on, Ravi. It'll be fun. I thought we were bonding," Margo said.

Jane lay down on the bed and rolled over six times before she got anywhere near the opposite edge. "Yeah, I don't mind sharing with you."

"I'll even sleep in the middle," Margo said. "Then you won't have to go anywhere near Jane's cooties."

"And what about your cooties?" Ravi asked, but there was something flirtatious in his delivery.

"I do not have cooties!" Margo said, hitting Ravi in the face with a pillow.

"Oh, I thought pillow fights only happened in movies," Ravi said, picking one up and smacking Margo lightly in the shoulder.

"See?" Margo said, settling down next to Jane. "This is going to be totally fun."

"Well, I think this has been worked out," Jane said, leaning back on the pillows and putting her hands behind her head. "Now let's see what's on basic cable this evening in Indiana."

"Excellent idea," Margo said.

"Fine," Ravi said, flopping down next to them. "This is a decent bed. Firm but not too firm. No springs in my back."

"I like it when you're pleasant," Margo said, punching his shoulder playfully.

"I can be pleasant. If I must."

Chapter 24

SLEEPING LATE WAS NOT AN OPTION THE NEXT MORNING. AS soon as one person woke up, everyone woke up.

"Well, that was the weirdest night of my life," Ravi said.

"What time is it?" Jane asked, rolling over and hugging her pillow.

"Like, seven," Margo said. "Better known as 'time to find Teo.'"

Jane jumped up at that and started getting ready.

"And breakfast. I think we should eat breakfast before Teo," Ravi said.

"But—" Jane started.

"Oh, come on, you said it yourself. It's not like he's being tortured. There's no reason we shouldn't have some waffles. Some bacon. Some eggs." Ravi got a far-off look in his eyes. "I just really like breakfast."

They got ready to go, and Ravi and Jane waited in the car while Margo checked out of the motel.

"I can't help feeling like he's going to be mad at me for telling you guys everything," Jane said, thinking aloud.

"I knew about the dad search."

"Yeah, but I told you a lot of stuff. Hopefully, he'll listen to reason."

"Teo normally . . . Wait! Why am I comforting you? Why does that keep happening?" He took a deep breath and turned back into normal Ravi. "I don't think you'll be able to talk your way out of this one."

Jane chewed on her lip, trying to ignore Ravi, but it was hard when the image of pissed-off Teo rose in her mind. He was so mad at her for getting involved in his dad search; what if he got just as mad that she had dragged Ravi and Margo into this?

"I know him very well," Ravi continued. "He'll be totally pissed."

"I'll just present the facts. Margo had to come because she is over eighteen, and you had to come because you're annoying and threatened to blackmail us. I think it makes perfect sense."

Margo got into the car a moment later, and they set off for a quick breakfast and then on to Champaign.

"Are you okay?" Margo asked, trying to decipher the look on Jane's face.

"She just realized that Teo is going to hate her after he finds out she betrayed his trust," Ravi explained.

"Aw, don't worry, Janie. You'll make him understand."

The closer they got, the less sure Jane was that Teo wouldn't be angry, but she had bigger things to deal with.

"All right, you guys stay in the car," Jane said as she drove onto campus and looked for a parking spot. "I think it'll be less weird if I go find Mateo alone."

"What are you going to tell him?" Margo asked.

"That I'm Teo's friend and I want to surprise him." Jane found a spot and parked.

"Good luck," Margo said.

Jane walked quickly across the campus, the skies growing darker and a storm threatening as she searched for the building she knew Mateo Rodriguez would be in, preparing to teach one of his last literature classes of the summer. She had a moment of panic, thinking there was a good chance he had canceled his final class.

Her panic disappeared when Jane found the classroom and saw the professor just about to walk in.

"Are you Mateo Rodriguez?" she asked, walking toward him.

"I am. What can I do for you?"

Jane immediately liked the way his eyes crinkled when he smiled. "Well, I'm Teo Garcia's, um . . ."

"Are you his girlfriend?" Mateo asked.

Jane was about to correct him but decided against it. "Did he say I was?" she asked.

"Well, I don't know who you are, so maybe?"

"Oh, I'm Jane. Jane Connelly."

"Nice to meet you."

Jane nodded.

"And for the record, he has spoken highly of you for the past two days."

Jane practically glowed. "Do you know where he is?"

"At my house."

"Do you mind telling me where you live? I feel weird asking, but I need to see him, and I drove all the way here. I'd be willing to wait until after class if that would make you feel more comfortable." Jane's babbling trailed off as Mateo scribbled his address on a scrap of paper.

"Thank you," she said.

"Are you going to try to talk some sense into him?"

"That's what I'm hoping," Jane said.

"Is Connie with you?"

Jane shook her head.

"Does Connie know where he is?"

"I don't think so."

"Oh God." He glanced into the classroom and then back at Jane. "Mostly today is just for handing in papers. I'll be there as soon as I can."

She nearly ran the whole way back to the car, which was easier said than done in a sundress and the flattest flip-flops ever made. Thunder was rolling overhead, not helping matters in the least, but she tried her best to ignore it.

She typed Mateo Rodriguez's address into the GPS, and the trio was on the way to his condo just as the skies opened up.

Once they got into the neighborhood, the condo development

was easy enough to find, even in a downpour. It was the individual condo that was an issue. It was in one of those impossible-to-navigate complexes that even confused the GPS.

"Turn right onto Birdsong Terrace," the GPS voice said.

"Make a sharp left to go north on Melody Drive."

"Yield to the left and then follow the road to keep right."

"Find a safe place to perform a U-turn."

"Drive off nearest cliff," Ravi said in a spot-on impression of the GPS voice's cadence.

When they finally pulled up in front of the right condo—or at least what they *hoped* was the right condo—Jane was tense enough to snap. She turned off the car's engine and prepared to slide out of the driver's seat.

"You guys wait here," she said.

For once, neither of her passengers complained. She must have really sounded like she meant business, if Ravi stayed quiet.

She rang the bell and stood on the front step under the small overhang and looked around, dripping wet and trying to ignore the lightning crackling in the distance. It was a nice-enough area. The lawns and bushes were well manicured. Teo wouldn't have to be on landscaper duty around here.

The door swung open and Teo stood on the other side.

"Jane?"

"That's me," she said.

"This is . . ."

Jane nodded.

"You're here. In a dress. In a thunderstorm."

"Yup, that's me."

"You're really here?"

Jane nodded, starting to shiver.

"You came to find me in a thunderstorm." He pulled her in for a hug just as lightning flashed behind her.

"I did," Jane said.

"Come on, get inside," he said, ushering her through the door and glancing back at her car parked at the curb.

"Is that Ravi and your sister in the car?" Teo asked, waving at them through the screen door.

"It's a long story," Jane said.

"Are they going to stay in the car, or are they allowed to come in?" Teo gestured for Ravi and Margo to come inside, and they ran to the front door.

They entered into a wide-open first-floor condo in which the living room flowed into the dining room flowed into the kitchen.

"Hey, Margo," Teo said.

Margo waved awkwardly.

"Hey, man," Teo said to Ravi. "It's good to see you, no matter how surprising it is that you're here."

"I missed you so much," Ravi said, pulling Teo into a hug.

"I understand," Teo said, patting him on the back.

"No, you don't. Last night was the worst night of my life. The three of us slept in the same bed. All three of us!"

"Was it a twin bed?" Teo asked Jane over Ravi's shoulder.

"No, it was huge. Definitely a king," Jane said.

Ravi finally let go of Teo and started wandering around the house, looking at all the photographs.

"You guys want anything?" Teo asked.

They all shook their heads. Jane shivered.

"I'll get you a towel," he said to her.

"Have a seat," he said when he got back.

They arranged themselves around the living room, Jane pulling the towel over her shoulders and drying the ends of her hair.

"What are you guys doing here?" Teo asked.

"After I read your last text, I got worried that you thought staying here was a legitimate plan. And you wouldn't answer my messages or take my calls, so I panicked."

"My phone was off."

"I kind of figured that out."

"And it *is* a legitimate plan," Teo said. "Maybe not one I'm totally sold on yet, but it's not crazy talk. It's possible."

"You can't stay here, Teo," Jane said.

"Why not?"

"What about school?" Margo asked.

"What about me?" Ravi asked.

"And does your uncle really want you to stay indefinitely?" Jane asked.

"He hasn't explicitly said anything on the subject," Teo replied.

"And even if you stay, you can't avoid your mom. You're under eighteen. She's going to have to give the okay on this." His face softened after Jane said that, so she kept going. "You'll have to see her again, no matter what. Even if you stayed here, you'd still have to see her. She would still be in your life. You're her child."

"I'll be eighteen in February," Teo said. But his argument was weaker somehow.

"It's a fun fantasy, Teo, but it can't magically happen with a snap of your fingers."

"And what about your sisters?" Ravi asked. "They're not quite as important as I am, but what would they think if you never came home?"

Teo smiled. "They'd hate me."

"Yeah, we'd all hate you."

"I don't know how I'm going to talk to my mom about all this," he said, choking up.

"It's all good," Ravi said. "Connie's cool. We know that. And maybe some of this is super messed up, but she's still your mom."

Teo looked so sad.

"Remember that time she took us to see that concert at PNC?" Ravi went on. "The salute to country music, because you were so in love with Carrie Underwood? Connie surprised you for your birthday. What mom does that? She loves you so freaking much she sat through the world's most annoying concert for her twelve-year-old son."

Before this, Jane had only seen outside Ravi, bold Ravi, too-much-to-say Ravi. This was a whole different kind of Ravi, talking Teo off the ledge. Jane couldn't believe how sensitive Ravi was when it came to Teo. How much he obviously cared about his friend. If he hadn't written *Jane Connelly is a B* on her locker in middle school, she might really respect him.

Around then, Mateo came in through the front door. After being introduced to everyone, he turned to Teo. "What's up?"

"My friends came to get me," Teo said.

"They did," Mateo said.

"They want me to go home with them."

"And what do you want?"

"I don't want to deal with my mom," Teo said. He sighed. "But I think I should probably go back with them."

"I think that's a good idea."

"I just don't know how to talk to my mom after everything you told me."

"I'm sure she had her reasons. Just remember that. Try to see it from her side."

"I'm a little too blinded by my own side."

"Just give her a chance, for me."

Teo took a deep breath and nodded. "Lemme get my backpack."

Ravi made small talk with Mateo while Teo was gone, and Jane wandered around, looking at the family photographs on the mantel. Even though Teo hadn't gotten a dad out of this mess, it looked like he was going to get a ton of new family members.

Saying good-bye to his uncle was obviously tough on Teo. "Thanks, Uncle Matt," he said as his uncle hugged him long and hard.

"Anytime. I mean, you're my namesake, man. I want to see

more of you. Just next time tell Connie where you are."

Teo nodded.

His uncle turned to the rest of the group. "Do you guys need anything for the road? Money? Food? Anything I can help you with?"

"No, we're good," Jane said. "We can keep running up the balance on Margo's credit card."

"And if we leave now, we might even make it home by midnight," Ravi said, faking enthusiasm.

Matt hugged each of them and then gave one last hug to Teo, as though he really didn't want his nephew to leave. Uncle Matt said something to him in Spanish, and then all four walked back to the car.

The sun was starting to come out by then, drying up the morning's rain.

"This sucks," Teo said.

"You wanna drive?" Jane asked. "Maybe that would cheer you up."

"Of course Teo gets to drive," Ravi muttered.

"Yeah, I think I'd like that," Teo said, ignoring Ravi.

Chapter 25

AS THEY SET OFF, TEO WAS CLEARLY UPSET. JANE TOOK HIS
hand from where it was resting on the gearshift.

"You okay?" she asked quietly, giving his hand a squeeze.

"Yeah," Teo said, swiping at his eyes.

"Margo is taking up more than half the backseat," Ravi
whined.

"I am not!" Margo said.

"Children, children," Jane said, using the same tone Margo
had employed the day before. "It's time to calm down and get
on the road." Then she turned back to Teo. "You sure you're okay
to drive?"

He had his face in his hands, and his shoulders were
shaking, but when he looked up, he was laughing instead of
crying. "How did you put up with them for the past two days?"

"It hasn't been easy—I'll tell you that much."

"Put up with *us*?" Ravi asked from the back. "As if. It was all about putting up with you and your sister and your stupid king-size-bed motel room."

"Did Ravi really just say 'as if'? Like he's Cher from *Clueless* or something?" Jane asked.

"I think he did," Margo said.

"*Clueless* is a highly underrated movie, and I have learned more about life and style from Murray than I have from anyone else. On earth."

"You know, Ravi, most guys would be psyched to share a bed with two girls," Margo said.

"Whatever," Ravi said, folding his arms and looking out the window. But there was a small smile on his face, because he had in fact shared a bed with two girls in one night. And maybe he could turn that into a much more interesting story while still having some basis in reality. Something to keep in mind for college.

Traffic was light as they set off, and they got to the state line in no time. "We're going to have to stop for gas sooner rather than later," Teo said, looking at the gauge.

"Yeah, and we can switch drivers because I can't take any more of your old-lady slowness," Margo said.

"*I* don't drive slow," Ravi said.

"I'm not letting you drive," Jane said.

"I'll take over. I promise to be careful," Margo said before Jane could object.

Teo pulled the car up by the gas tanks. The rest stop was low on amenities—just restrooms and vending machines.

Margo and Ravi were ready to go a few minutes later, but Teo was nowhere to be found. Jane came back out with her hands full of vending-machine snacks.

"Where's Teo?" Margo asked as Jane slid into the backseat and dumped her snacks in the middle.

"He's not out here?" Jane asked, worried enough by his disappearance that she didn't even complain about Ravi's stealing the front seat.

"We thought he was with you," Margo said.

"Stay here and I'll go look," Jane said.

She found Teo around the back of the rest stop, looking out over a ravine with a brook at the bottom.

"Don't jump," Jane said.

"I can't believe you came to rescue me," Teo said, ignoring Jane's lame attempt at a joke. "You didn't have to, but you did."

"Are we talking about right now?"

"You know what I'm talking about."

"It wasn't really a rescue."

"It was still amazing, and, I don't know, it's like you rescued me from myself." He shook his head. "And you did it in a thunderstorm."

"It's not a big deal."

He turned to face her. "How about you accept the compliment, Jane? You're awesome and smart. There aren't very many people in the world who would do something like this for me."

"Well, there are at least three."

"Yeah, I feel like we haven't covered that properly. Why *is* Margo here?"

"She's the money."

"Makes sense." Teo looked thoughtful. "So Ravi came because he's Ravi, and Margo came because she's the money, but why did you come, Jane?"

Jane shrugged. "You know why I came."

"Your love for road trips?"

"Yeah, let's go with that."

"Come on. I need to hear you say it."

"Fine," Jane said, shoulders slumping. "I couldn't deal with the idea that you weren't coming home. Even if you weren't serious about it. Even if you were just blowing off steam. If I didn't come see you and try to change your mind, I would always wonder if I could have made a difference."

"You could have called," he said, grinning.

"I did call! You had your phone off!" Jane said, throwing her hands in the air.

"I know, I know."

"Have you turned it back on?"

Teo slipped his hand into hers. "I'm not there yet. That would be facing reality."

Jane nodded.

"I'm glad you're here," Teo said.

"Then I'm glad I'm here, too."

"What am I going to say to my mom?"

"I don't know," Jane said.

"What would the Magic 8 tell me?" Teo asked, pretending to hold it in his free hand.

"Well, ignoring the fact that you haven't asked a yes-or-no question, I don't know. But I have it in the car."

"You brought it along?"

"I didn't know whether I might need a quick consultation on the road."

"And did you?"

Jane shook her head. "I've needed it less and less lately. Things haven't seemed as daunting for the past few weeks."

"Why do you think that is?"

"I could hazard a guess."

Teo smiled, and Jane decided not to wait even one more minute. She stood on her tiptoes just wanting to peck his lips, but it quickly turned into more.

Jane wasn't sure what she'd expected, but she was surprised by Teo's hunger. She was so wrapped up in his chin, his lips, his skin, and the way they were all working together and making her *feel* that she forgot to respond for a second.

Teo was about to pull away because seconds felt like minutes when the person being kissed wasn't responding. But then Jane put a hand on his cheek, feeling a little bit of stubble, and smiled into Teo's mouth.

It felt like all the tension, frustration, and attraction that had been building between them all summer was bursting out of their pores in a shower of sparks.

Ravi chose that moment to come around the side of the building. "Ah! My eyes. Someone pass me the brain bleach."

"I'm sorry about him," Teo said, pulling away with a sigh.

"It's okay. I think I'm starting to come to terms with his existence," Jane said as they walked in Ravi's direction. Teo took her hand and didn't drop it until they got to the car and he was distracted by the three different varieties of Fritos she had purchased.

She'd probably pick Fritos over Teo, too, she told herself.

She also told herself that it was well worth sitting in the backseat of your own car if it meant you had the chance to lean your head on the shoulder of the boy you liked while you drove home from rescuing him from himself.

It was a complicated thought, but one Jane stood by.

She slept on and off, waking up and smiling at the feel of Teo's arm around her. No matter how bad things might get at home, for either one of them, she was glad to have this time.

Even the low hum of Margo and Ravi's incessant arguing—about everything from gas mileage to politics to movies—felt right.

Ravi's phone rang.

"Don't answer it!" Jane cried, yanking herself out of her stupor and sitting up.

Too late.

"Hi, Mommy."

"He calls his mom 'Mommy' on the regular?" Jane asked Teo.

Teo nodded.

Jane could hear the murmur of Ravi's mom's voice on the other end.

"I'll be home soon. I'm at Teo's."

His mom's even tone turned up a notch.

"Oh. Ah. Yeah. We're—" Ravi didn't finish that sentence because his mother started yelling.

"Fine. We're about two hours away."

More yelling.

"Yes. I'll meet you at the Connellys'." Ravi hung up. "So everyone is at your house," he said, turning to Jane. "And they know where we've been."

"How did they find out we were gone?" Jane asked.

"They checked Margo's credit card."

"Yeah, I figured that would happen," Margo said. "I just didn't want to ruin the fun."

The rest of the car ride was quiet as all of them prepared themselves for the inevitable shitstorm that awaited them.

In what seemed like no time at all, they were parked in Jane's driveway.

"I guess we need to do this," she said, getting out of the car along with Margo and Ravi.

Teo got out, too, and hugged Ravi. "Thanks for coming, man," he said.

"Anytime. Except maybe next time we go on a road trip, Jane doesn't have to be involved."

"Jane's gonna be involved. You have to come to terms with Jane's involvement."

"Fine. But I don't like her."

"You don't have to," Teo said. "In fact, if you did, we'd probably have to have some words."

Jane took a deep breath.

Teo squeezed her shoulder. "We got this."

"I hope you're right," Jane said.

"I hate getting into trouble," Margo said.

"It's okay—at least you get to go back to college," Teo said. "I've been gone three days without talking to my mom even once. She's probably going to kill me."

"We're all definitely in trouble," Jane said as the front door opened. First Ravi's mom came out, and then Connie. Jane and Margo's parents stood in the doorway.

Ravi's mom grabbed his ear. "What were you thinking?" she asked.

"Teo needed my help!"

She shook her head and dragged him to her car. Ravi waved sadly from the passenger seat as she drove away.

"Teo! Oh my God, Teo," Connie said. "I can't believe you're here."

"Yeah, Ma. I'm here," he said.

She kissed every inch of his face and then smacked him in the arm and started speaking Spanish so fast that not even Teo could keep up.

"Yeah, I gotta go," Teo said to Jane and Margo.

"We'll talk," Jane said, wishing she could kiss him good-bye.

"I'll call you," Teo said.

"No, he won't," Connie said.

But as Teo and his mom walked down the street, he looked back and held up his hand in an *I'll call* gesture. Jane believed him. He'd find a way, no matter what Connie said.

Chapter 26

CONNIE AND TEO WENT THROUGH THE BACK DOOR. BUCK was leaning on the kitchen counter with a half-eaten sandwich next to him.

"So how is everyone?" he asked. "Anything I can do to help?"

Both Connie and Teo glared at him.

"Okay, well, if anyone needs me, I'll be upstairs," Buck said, backing out of the kitchen so fast that he left his sandwich behind.

"All right, let's get this over with," Connie said in Spanish.

"Oh, now you want to speak Spanish?" Teo asked in English.

"What's that supposed to mean?"

"We used to speak Spanish all the time, and then we stopped. You're not even teaching the girls to speak it."

Her mouth dropped open, but she recovered. "That has nothing to do with this."

"Of course it does," Teo said.

"What were you thinking?" his mom asked, ignoring his previous remark.

"I was thinking that you never told me the truth, and I need to know the truth," Teo answered. "I was thinking that you don't listen to me. And that you're still not listening to me."

"You need to trust your mother is what you need to do," she said, her voice rising.

"Maybe you should be quieter unless you want the girls to wake up," Teo said.

"I will speak as loudly as I want in my own home!" she yelled. "I will not be reprimanded by my son, who has done nothing but lie to me."

"I had no choice!" Teo yelled back.

"What am I going to do with you, Teo?" she asked, putting her hands up in surrender.

He rolled his eyes and crossed his arms, leaning against the kitchen island.

"You must have something else to say for yourself. How did this happen?"

"Jane found him for me. I'd been sort of idly looking for my dad for years, but I never found anything. Then Jane learned about my search, and the next thing I knew, she had all this information on Mateo Rodriguez."

"But why wouldn't you ask me?"

"Seriously?"

"Of course."

"I would have asked you. I did ask you. But for so long you told me we were happy. You told me we didn't need anyone else, just you and me. Every time I would ask you about my dad, you would say we were enough for each other. Me and you."

"We *were* happy—"

"Mom, please," Teo said. "I gotta get this out."

"Sorry." She swiped at her eyes with the back of her hand and grabbed for a napkin.

"And then you married Buck. All I could think was that if we were so happy, then why did we need Buck? It sort of festered for a few years. I didn't understand it or even acknowledge it, but it was there—this weird feeling of anger mixed with rejection."

"I never meant to make you feel that way," she whispered.

"Well, you did."

"I am sorry, Teo, that you had to find out about Jose this way."

"Sure, now you're sorry." Teo's anger flared like fire, as if he couldn't contain it anymore. "Why didn't you tell me sooner?"

She stepped up to him and put her hands on his arms, looking him straight in the eye.

"I thought I was protecting you," she said.

And that was what sent Teo over the edge.

"From what?" he asked, pulling himself out of her grasp. "You were keeping me from knowing my family. There's a whole family for me there. Aunts and uncles and cousins and grandparents. I wanted all that my whole life, and you kept them from me."

"I was protecting me, too," she said.

"How was that fair to me?" he asked, his voice growing louder, all pretense of civility forgotten.

"I was trying to be fair to both of us. I was young. I didn't have any money. I worried that they would want you, particularly after Jose passed away."

"But they couldn't just do that."

"Maybe they could, and maybe they couldn't. But the idea that they might was enough to frighten me."

"Is that why you weren't with him before?"

"I wasn't with him because I knew he was the kind of man who would want to get married."

"And that would have been so terrible?" Teo bit out.

"I wasn't looking for a husband when I was nineteen. Jose and I were always tumultuous. I didn't want to marry him. I liked his edge, but I didn't want to be with him forever. And if he knew about you, he would have wanted to make it forever."

"It was selfish," Teo said. His tone was even now, but his heart was racing.

"It was."

"And then you were even more selfish when you married Buck and still kept me away from that part of my family." Teo pounded his chest with his fist.

"I thought Buck could be our family, yours and mine. His

family loves you, his parents and his brother. The girls love you and I love you."

"I know, but—" Teo stood up and started pacing. "Maybe that's not enough. Once you had what you wanted, why couldn't I have what I wanted?"

She looked ashamed. "I believed I would have less."

"Less what? Now you've ended up with so much more, and I have almost nothing."

"How do you have less? Do you hear yourself?"

"I wanted aunts, uncles, cousins, and grandparents. I wanted relatives. And they're all there waiting for me on that side of the family. I look like them. I sound like them. We go to Buck's family stuff, and all I can see is how *other* I am."

"I'm other, too."

"Yeah. But you're Buck's wife, the mother of Buck's children. I'm this weird familial leech. Like, 'Oh, look at Connie's son. I hear he doesn't even have a father.'"

"No one is saying that."

"But they're thinking it."

"No one is thinking that, Teo. No one is judging you." Her face was soft and kind, making Teo feel even angrier.

"It feels like they are," he said, running his hands through his hair and pacing.

"That's something we'll have to work on together. I wish I could change how you feel, but I can only promise to try to help you."

Teo nodded.

"Unfortunately, we have more pressing things to deal with right now."

Teo narrowed his eyes at her.

"We need to discuss your punishment."

"Why am I being punished for your mistakes?"

"You're being punished for lying and running away. This could have all been avoided if you'd just talked to me about it."

"Why aren't you getting this? I used to try to talk to you about this all the time. You would shut me down."

"So what is it you want from me?"

"I want to see my family."

"I never said you couldn't."

"You sort of implied it by not telling me they exist," he said.

"I won't stop you now. Not anymore."

"I'm sure you'll think of ways to keep me from them."

"Give me a little bit of credit."

He stared at her. "No," he said simply.

Then he turned and ran out the back door. He didn't stop running until he was around the corner.

Chapter 27

"OH GOD, OH BOY, I CAN'T HANDLE THIS. WE'RE GOING TO BE in so much trouble," Margo whispered hysterically in Jane's ear as they approached the front door.

"Chill out, Margo," Jane snapped.

"I can't chill out," Margo said. "I'm way beyond chilling out ever again."

Jane sighed.

"Welcome home, girls," their mom said in a scarily saccharine voice.

"Come on," their dad said, moving aside to let them into the house.

Their parents escorted them into the dining room, where they took their usual seats at the table.

"What on earth do you have to say for yourself?"

their mother asked Jane.

"Um, well, here's the thing..." Jane said, trying to stall, trying to come up with an excuse that would lighten her sentence, even though she knew she would basically be grounded forever, no matter what. She was prepared to take it like an adult, whatever they threw at her. She'd known what she was getting herself into.

"I'm bisexual," Margo said.

Jane turned to her sister, incredulous. "Now you decide to tell them?" Jane blurted out.

Margo shook her head a little, trying to get Jane to shut up, hoping to spare her by taking the brunt of the explosion.

"What?" their mom asked.

"What does that have to do with driving halfway across the country?" their dad asked.

"Well, nothing, but I wanted you to know that I like guys and girls."

"Okay, processing," their dad said.

"That's nice, Margo. I'm glad you feel like you can be honest with us," their mom said, turning to look at Jane. "Unlike your sister, who thought it was a good idea to drive to Indiana—"

"Illinois, technically," Jane said automatically.

"Unnecessary correction, Jane," their dad said.

"To *Illinois*," their mom continued. "To pick up Teo. What were you thinking?"

"Don't you think we should talk about Margo's thing for a while?"

"I think there's plenty of time to do that later. Right now we need to understand what you were thinking the past few days," their dad said.

"We weren't thinking," Jane said. "Or Margo wasn't. She was just along for the ride. I needed help, and I persuaded her to come along."

"No, I wanted to go," Margo said. "It's not like Jane brainwashed me."

Their father scratched his head. "So take me through this. What exactly happened?"

Jane explained the whole story for her parents. She was getting a little tired of telling it, but she knew she needed to get through it at least one more time, because she owed them an explanation. Maybe they would lighten the sentence when they realized she'd been trying to help Teo out.

"Too much information," their dad said, shaking his head.

"Jane," their mom began, clearly disappointed. She was like a caricature of disappointment. "Lying? Driving across state lines? Just to pick up Teo? He was in enough trouble on his own. There was absolutely no reason to get involved."

"He wasn't going to come back," Margo said, stepping in. "Jane was really worried that he wouldn't come back on his own. And I'm not surprised she was worried. He's kind of a mess."

"But there was no reason for you girls to get involved!" their mother yelled.

"I like him," Jane said, her voice even, trying to keep things from escalating. "A lot. Enough to risk getting into trouble. I wanted him to come back. I knew he had to come back. And I knew that if I went and got him, he'd see that there really wasn't any other choice."

"You should have left this to Connie and Buck," their mom said through gritted teeth.

"Maybe or maybe not," Jane said. "Did you know Teo's dad is dead?"

Their mom started to answer, then stopped short and glanced at her husband. "Yes."

He put two fingers to each temple and rubbed. "What is going on in my life right now?" he asked, closing his eyes.

"I know, Pops. It's a lot to take in," Margo said.

"So many secrets." He sat up. "I kind of wish I had one to share."

He looked at his wife for a second, sharing some kind of silent conversation, and then they turned their attention back to their daughters.

"Thank you for telling us about yourself, Margo. We appreciate it. We love you and we support you, no matter what," their dad said. "We can't condone what you did, and you will have to pay back the charges on your credit card, which Jane will help with, but that's the end of it. How can we ground a twenty-year-old? It's ridiculous."

"Thanks, Dad," Margo said.

"Jane," their mother said, shaking her head. "This is unacceptable. I think it's fair to ground you for as long we deem reasonable."

"What's reasonable?" Jane asked.

"Your mother and I still need to discuss that," their father said.

"Can I at least talk to Teo? Make sure he's okay?"

Their parents looked at each other. "We'll have to talk about that, too. You can't just run off whenever you like," their dad said, looking at Jane.

"I know," she said. "This was important, though. I swear it was. I thought it was the only way to get Teo back."

Margo nodded in solidarity. Looking at their mother's set jaw, she decided not to get more involved than that.

Their mother shook her head slowly. "Definitely no seeing Teo."

Jane's eyes narrowed.

Their dad put his hand on his wife's shoulder. "Jane," he said, "I know this is tough. The older you get, the more you think you're smart enough to make all your own decisions. But I promise you still need us. We're not useless. You should have come to us. And that's why you're in trouble. Not only for making us worry like crazy for the past two days, but because you didn't give us the benefit of the doubt."

"Maybe you need to give me the benefit of the doubt, too," Jane said. "I deserve to have some say in my own life."

"Why? You've barely shown any interest—" their mom began.

"Because it's my life and you need to trust me," Jane said, cutting her off.

Their mother whipped her head up to look at Jane. "What you

need to realize is that you're not the adult here. You need to spend more time deciding your future and worrying less about Teo."

"How can you tell me in one sentence that I'm not an adult, but in the next sentence tell me that I need to make adult decisions? Why does no one else see the flaw in this logic?" Jane asked. The anger she had been trying to keep at bay started to rise.

Their dad's jaw dropped, but their mother was right on top of Jane's question. "This is adolescence, Jane. This isn't adulthood. You need to make decisions now, while we can help guide you, and while there is still time to make changes if those decisions don't work out."

"If anything can be changed later, why do I have to make these decisions now? Can't I just do what I want for now?"

"And what is it you want?"

"Not to go to college. Not to waste my time and your money on some useless degree in a subject that I'm not very interested in."

"What *are* you interested in?"

"I don't know," Jane said. She didn't understand why that was so difficult for her parents to grasp. "I don't know what I want to do. I just know a few things that I *don't* want to do. Why can't I explore for a while? Why can't I take my time?"

"What does that even mean?" their mother asked, rubbing her face with her hands.

"I can find a job and roommates and figure things out. I don't want to go to college just because everyone is supposed to go to college."

"This is the wrong time for this conversation," their mother said.

"Then when's the right time? You've been trying to push me into this discussion all summer. I'm ready now. When's the right time, Mom? When you say so?"

"We have other things to deal with right now. We need to talk about your poor choices and what happened. If you would just try to get into a good school, like Margo did, we wouldn't have to deal with this."

"What? So I can make mistakes like getting involved in a pyramid scheme?"

"Hey!" Margo said. Jane grimaced at her.

"Oh, that's old news, Jane. Margo has grown so much since then," their mom said.

"But you always take her side! Margo never does anything wrong."

"This isn't about Margo. This is about you."

Jane was so frustrated she could scream.

"No," Jane said, shaking her head. "I think this is about *you*, Mom."

"What?"

"This is about what *you* want and what *you* think I should do. You want me to make decisions about my future, but only ones that *you* approve of. This is about your double standard."

"There isn't a double standard," their mother said.

"Maybe not from where you're sitting, but definitely from where I'm sitting."

"This is ridiculous."

"The only thing that's ridiculous is that you won't let me make my own mistakes."

"I need to save you from terrible choices and poor decision making."

Jane felt her nostrils flare. In that moment she wished she could breathe fire.

Instead, she stood up from the table, held her head high, and walked out the front door.

Chapter 28

JANE AND TEO WERE SO STUCK IN THEIR OWN THOUGHTS that they almost walked into each other on the sidewalk.

"Stormed out?" Jane asked.

"Yup," Teo said.

"Me too."

They started walking in the direction of the park. When they were halfway there, Jane's hand found Teo's and held on tight.

"So is your mom literally going to kill you?" Jane asked.

"I have no freaking clue," he said.

"Are you guys going to be okay?"

Teo shrugged.

"We don't have to talk about this right now," Jane said.

"Good idea."

"My mom talked to Uncle Matt. He called her this afternoon."

"Oh, so Mateo tattled on us."

"Yup, he's the one. Him and the credit card company."

Jane smiled into the darkness as they got to the park. The only light came from a streetlamp reflecting off the surface of the pond as they took a seat on one of the bench swings nearby.

Teo pushed off with his toes, making the swing sway gently. "I think I might apply to the University of Illinois at Urbana-Champaign. I want to get to know Mateo and that whole side of the family. I hadn't settled on a school anyway, and I actually think I have a really good shot of getting in."

"I still have no clue what to do about college, but I'll figure it out."

"You could always come with me."

"You're just saying that because you need someone, not because you want me there."

"Jane, you're not a placeholder. You're so much more than that to me."

"Were you serious today when you said I was smart?" Jane asked, leaning back and putting her head on his shoulder.

"Of course I was serious. You're brilliant, even. You're so levelheaded," Teo said.

"I just needed to hear it."

"I'll tell you every single day until you believe me."

"I wish we didn't have to go home."

"I know. I'm still not sure how to deal with my mom. She's been lying to me for years. How can I trust her?"

"Maybe you need to stop listening to what she's saying and try to read between the lines," Jane said.

"Maybe." Teo stared at the ground.

"She's smart, your mom. She might have done some shitty stuff and maybe didn't make all the right decisions, but she's smarter than I am. I know that for sure. And if you trust me, then maybe you should trust her."

"I used to trust her. Now I'm not so sure. Now I don't know who to trust."

"Me. Probably Ravi. Margo in a pinch. Your sisters. Your mom. Maybe even Buck."

"I get it," Teo said. "I just need a little longer to believe it, I guess."

"I can help you with that."

"You're going to tutor me?"

"Sure thing. I'm a genius according to you," Jane said.

"Okay, smarty-pants, what are you going to do about your parents?"

"Accept that I'm grounded forever and take my punishment like an adult. After all, I did leave the state without their permission and dropped a trail of lies in my wake."

"Yeah, you do sound smarter than me."

They were quiet for a minute after that, watching the ripples of water in the pond and enjoying what would likely be their last few moments of freedom.

"We should probably get going." Jane sighed.

Teo nodded and they stood up, heading in the direction of home. He put his arm around her shoulders as they walked.

"It's funny. . . . Just as my parents were getting ready to really start yelling, Margo tried to rescue me by coming out of the closet," Jane said.

Teo stepped back and looked at her, confused. "Margo was in the closet?"

Jane put a hand over her mouth. "I don't know if I'm supposed to tell people that. Maybe only Margo's supposed to tell people."

"The cat's kind of already out of the bag."

"True," Jane said, thinking it over. "So yeah, Margo's bisexual."

Teo slapped a hand to his forehead. "I thought I saw her making out with Kara Maxwell behind the pool one day, but I wasn't sure it was her. I didn't recognize her."

"She never told me she made out with Kara Maxwell behind the pool!"

"She totally did."

As they approached Jane's house, they saw two people talking on the front steps. Two people who just so happened to be their respective moms.

Teo squeezed Jane's hand, and Jane squeezed back.

"Well, look who decided to come back," Connie said.

"Sorry," Jane said.

Connie stood up. "It's okay, Jane."

"We were just about to go after you," Jane's mom said, her

voice sounding lighter than it had in months, particularly considering the circumstances.

Jane snuck a peek at her mom. "I'm sorry I left."

"Me too," Teo said, addressing both moms. "I'm sorry about everything."

Jane's mom looked at her. "We're sorry we didn't listen, and we're going to work on that."

"Yeah?" Jane asked.

Her mom nodded, and Jane could see tears in her eyes.

"Connie and I talked about it. You're both still in a lot of trouble—even more because you ran away in the middle of your sentencing—but we'll have plenty of time to discuss it all while you're both under house arrest until school starts."

Jane and Teo sighed in unison. There wasn't even anything to protest.

"And we'll even give you a minute to say good-bye," Connie said.

Jane's mom slipped into the house, and Connie walked in the direction of hers.

"So," Jane said, "how do we make the most of this?"

"I don't know," Teo said.

There was too much to say and do and not enough time for any of it with their moms keeping tracking of the clock. It seemed like a second later when Jane's mom knocked on the window to let them know their time was up.

"I guess I'd better go," Teo said.

Jane nodded and turned to go inside. Teo leaped into action, catching her from behind and spinning her around, pressing his lips to hers and drinking her in.

"Now, why didn't I think of that?" Jane asked into his mouth.

Teo smiled. "You were just letting me be the brains of the operation for once."

"For once," Jane agreed as Teo backed up and started toward his house.

Jane stood on her front walk and watched Teo until he was at the corner. Before he was out of sight, he turned back one last time.

He cupped his hands around his mouth and yelled, "Can you ask your Magic 8 Ball if you are my girlfriend?"

"Signs point to yes," Jane called back.

Acknowledgments

First of all, mega thanks to Holly West. Through every draft, every obstacle, every brainstorming phone call, and every terrible idea, she was there to guide me back to the point. This book would not exist without her encouragement and optimism.

Tons of gratitude to the Swoon staff as a whole: Jean Feiwel, Alison Verost, Kathryn Little, Caitlin Sweeny, and Lauren Scobell have made this a truly amazing experience. And to my favorite travel companions, Nicole Banholzer and Brittany Pearlman: Thanks for making seven cities in eight days much easier to deal with. To my fellow Swoon authors: I love how much this group has grown, and I'm so glad we're in it together!

To my friends at the Morristown & Morris Township Library: Thanks for not making me feel too guilty about leaving. To the kids in the tenth- to twelfth-grade book club during the summer of 2014, thanks for all your help! Without you guys, this story would have never even seen the light of day and Teo wouldn't be a lifeguard.

Endless amounts of appreciation to Lauren Velella, who

holds the title of being the only person besides Holly to read every single draft of this one. Next time I talk to you, I will whistle the theme song to *The Golden Girls* in its entirety as a show of thanks.

Sometimes all you need is a kind ear, so thank you to Michelle Petrasek and Chrissy George for always listening cheerfully even when I've rambled endlessly about absolutely nothing. And to Kate Vasilik, Katie Nellen, Chelsea Reichert, and Melanie Morritt for lots of things, but particularly for reminding me that I shouldn't send a character named Margo on a road trip to Florida for fear of people drawing comparisons to a different book.

A great big heap of thanks to my aunt and uncle, Brenda and Bill Bankos, who have been unbelievably excited and genuinely wonderful through this whole experience.

The niblings already got their moment at the beginning of the book, so I'll skip them this time, but thanks to my siblings, Karen, Scott, and Sean, and my siblings-in-law, Bill and Sandra.

I would need to make a whole new word to accurately express how thankful I am to my mom, Pat, who's been so supportive and understanding as I dive into my writing career, so we'll just leave it with thanks, and I'll work on the new vocabulary before the next book. And to my dad, Wayne, who I know would be so proud.

© Susana Ramirez

Sandy Hall is the author of *A Little Something Different* and *Signs Point to Yes*. She is a teen librarian from New Jersey, where she was born and raised, and has a BA in Communication and a Master of Library and Information Science from Rutgers University. When she isn't writing or teen librarian–ing, she enjoys reading, marathoning TV shows, and taking long scrolls through Tumblr.

sandywrites.tumblr.com

Turn the page for some

Sw♥♥nworthy

Extras...

Jane's List of Doctor Who Episodes that Teo MUST Watch

(Some of these are two-parters and NO I do not think that's cheating.)

1. Blink

I insist that you watch this episode. No one can resist this episode. Even the staunchest anti-*Who* lobbyists would be willing to watch this episode, mostly because the Doctor is barely even in it.

2. Vincent and the Doctor

This episode is one of my favorites because it's not just about how the Doctor is helping Vincent van Gogh OF ALL PEOPLE, but also because he's really helping Amy. She's so sad, and he really does take her mind off it. Also all the incredible art you get to see. And Bill Nighy! I love that guy.

3. The Angels Take Manhattan

A WORLD OF CREEPINESS. When the Statue of Liberty starts walking around, you know you're in trouble. I love River Song in this episode. And I'm hoping when you see River Song you'll have enough questions to make you want to keep watching.

4. The Empty Child/The Doctor Dances

"Are you my mummy?" I think I'm really drawn to the scarier/weirder episodes. This one is both scary and weird. But it has a happy ending! Oh, and Captain Jack Harkness! I love him and I think you will, too! Side note: I do hope that by the time we get to these two episodes you'll be willing to watch the whole series, but if not, I'm ready with more choice examples, so that at the very least you can discuss certain things with me.

5. The Runaway Bride

I love Donna, so sue me! I love this introduction of her, and I love that we

don't even see her again for a full season. But after all that Rose business (Don't get me started on Rose—I can hardly talk about her, and that's why she's not featured often on this list. My pain is too real.) at the end of series two, this episode felt like a breath of fresh air. I was delighted by all those Santas with guns, too.

6. The Impossible Astronaut

This episode is brilliant, and I will fight anyone who disagrees.

7. The Eleventh Hour

The premier episode of my favorite Doctor? Of course it's on this list. I'll never look at fish fingers and custard the same way.

8. The Lodger

The Doctor gets locked out of the Tardis, and he goes to live with a random dude named Craig. Hilarity ensues. And there's a creepy upstairs room, which is always a bonus!

9. New Earth

I'm putting this on the list so you get a decent taste of Ten and Rose. Lots of people love them. I did. UNTIL THEY RIPPED MY HEART OUT AND KICKED IT TO THE CURB. But it's a quality episode, and there's this whole thing with cat people and body swapping, and you can't go wrong with any of that.

10. Silence in the Library/Forest of the Dead

BECAUSE OF DONNA AND HOW MUCH I LOVE HER. NOT TO MENTION THE CREEPINESS. I wish I could someday get through a list of favorite anything without turning into a screaming, emotional fangirl about this show, but today is apparently not that day. I apologize for the misuse of caps lock. It is the only way I can express my feelings.

Signs Point to YES

Discussion Questions

1. Jane lucked out with her random babysitting job. What is the best summer job you ever had? Worst?

2. Jane plans to get a job instead of going to college, and figure things out from there. What do you think about this?

3. Teo feels like an outsider in his own family. Have you ever felt like this? If so, how did you deal with that?

4. Jane loves *Doctor Who* and writing fan fiction. Have you ever participated in fandom or reading/writing fan fiction?

5. Jane wishes she could sink through the floor after mentioning Teo's "boy nipples." Have you ever said or done something awkward in front of a crush?

6. Jane asks her Magic 8 Ball for advice and loves doing "cinematic serendipity." Do you have any superstitions? Do you prefer to wing it or have definite plans?

7. Margo is terrified of coming out to her family. What advice would you give her?

8. Ravi has held a grudge against Jane for many years. Have you ever held a grudge like that?

9. After Teo tells Jane he's not coming back, Jane jumps in the car to go get him. What would you have done?

10. Do you agree with Connie's decision not to tell Teo about Jose? Or do you feel Teo's reaction was justified?

Swoon Reads

A Coffee Date

with author Sandy Hall and her editor, Holly West

"Getting to Know You (a Little More!)"

Holly West (HW): What is your favorite word?

Sandy Hall (SH): Have we talked about this? Did you know to ask this question? Because I have five favorite words. They are *haberdashery*, *insouciant*, *ennui*, *winsome*, and *ineffable*.

HW: I like them. They're so fun to say.

SH: They are! And all of them—aside from *haberdashery*, which is just sort of a really fun word—I really love to use all of them. *Insouciant* means "nonchalant." But it's not a nonchalant word! And *ennui* . . . it's just great.

HW: *Ennui* is great.

SH: So yeah, I have five favorite words. I'm so happy you have no idea. I just love words. Oh, I also love *pulchritudinous*, which is the ugliest word for meaning "attractive."

HW: Do you have any strange or funny habits? And if not now, when you were a kid?

SH: To this day, I can only eat candy in even numbers. I hate eating candy in odd numbers. I hate it. Like if I have one Altoid? No, I have two. If I have a Skittle? No, eighteen.

HW: I love that you count them.

SH: No, I do. I do. It is sort of all part of my bribery with my word count and stuff. It is sort of all part of that, but it's been going on my whole life.

Swoon Reads

I really just love to eat candy in even numbers. And I only like even numbers. I'm a little turned off by odd numbers.

HW: Interesting. I like multiples of five.
SH: I do like multiples of five. My birthday is the fifteenth. I feel okay about the number fifteen. But in general I shy away from odd numbers.

"The Swoon Reads Experience (Continues!)"

HW: Did publishing *A Little Something Different* change your life?
SH: Absolutely! In the best way possible. I got to quit my full-time job. But aside from that, it's just amazing getting to meet so many people. It's amazing feeling like I'm doing something that I really want to do. And I really do love being a librarian. I wouldn't be doing it part-time now if I didn't really love being a librarian. But the way writing happened and becoming an author and getting published happened just felt very natural, and I'm super thrilled to be here.

HW: What's your favorite thing so far—because we hope to have many more books—about being a Swoon Reads author?
SH: Probably Holly. No, and I'm not even really joking. You make this all very easy, and I like having you as my point person and I can ask you every dumb question. Because I don't have an agent, and I am very new at this, so you never make me feel stupid. And I do love my other authors. Even if we're just Internet friends, I feel like I have a good, nice group that supports each other.

HW: *blushing* I love the Swoon Reads support group. It's awesome. So we sent you on tour for *A Little Something Different*. What was the oddest thing that happened?

Swoon Reads

SH: You know, I think I'm so new at this that everything's been just really nice and genuine. As a fangirl, I know I would say something super ridiculous if I met Darren Criss. But nothing super odd has happened. The weirdest thing was my roommate from college came to one of my signings and she brought me this huge wicker squirrel. I was like, "What am I going to do with this?!" It was awesome. But I had to FedEx it home because it wouldn't fit in my suitcase. I'm hoping for lots of Magic 8 Balls out of this book. Or maybe they'll give me *Doctor Who* stuff!

HW: That could be good. You could get fandom stuff out of it!
SH: I could work on that swag!

HW: Do you have any advice for aspiring authors on Swoon Reads?
SH: Listen to what people say to you. Read the comments, and read comments on other people's books. Even on books that you're not necessarily reading, read every comment you can find. Read every blog post. Take in all the information you can imagine. And don't be afraid to promote yourself to your friends, your family, on Twitter. . . . I always see Swoon Reads will retweet when somebody says, "Check out my book on the site!" And you know what? Sometimes that's all it takes, and it's right there in front of you and someone wants to click on it. Promote yourself. Give yourself a leg up.

"The Next Phase of the Writing Life"

HW: Was the editing process different for you this time around?
SH: Yes, because I thought you were going to fire me. [Laughs]

HW: We were not going to fire you!
SH: It was different. For this book, I didn't have quite the same vision for it that I had for *A Little Something Different*. It wasn't written in a vacuum.

Swoon Reads

It was pushed more, let's say. In my head. I had to push at it. It didn't just write itself. It wasn't some kind of magical moment. And I kept waiting for some magical "eureka!" moment, and nothing ever came. Until the brainstorming phone call where we changed "Benj" to "Teo" and everything finally clicked into place!

HW: Where did you get your inspiration for *Signs Point to Yes*?
SH: From high school book club last summer. A lot of it came from them. I love, love, love neighborhood friendship, and people who were friends as kids who lose touch. I think almost everybody could tell you about a boy who lived in their neighborhood, who they played with when they were eight and then never talked to again. It's amazing that you still live in the same neighborhood, and you still go to high school together, and your parents still talk to each other, but you just never cross paths. I just really like that idea. And the kids gave me a lot of, "Oh, what if he's a lifeguard?" and "What if she's this?" And they all loved *Doctor Who*, so that's how that got brought in.

HW: If you could have a reader remember one thing about your book, what would that be?
SH: Well, for *A Little Something Different*, I always, always, always just want people to think about how you have no idea what's going on in someone else's head. You could never, ever guess what's happening in their life or behind the scenes. I think people can get way too wrapped up in what they're seeing—and I know I do it—and not take in the full scope of things. I think for *Signs Point to Yes*, I'd like to go with "Don't compare yourself to other people." You're going to do, in your time, what you want to do. I think that's what Jane learned throughout the book, even if it's not written out on the page. She didn't have to be like Margo; she didn't have to be what her mom wanted her to be. There's no measuring stick.